DO NOT REMOVE
CARDS FROM POCKET

Love is
a time of enchantment:
in it all days are fair and all fields
green. Youth is blest by it,
old age made benign: the eyes of love see
roses blooming in December,
and sunshine through rain. Verily
is the time of true-love
a time of enchantment—and
Oh! how eager is woman
to be bewitched!

DAWN OF DELIGHT

Gemma's whole life revolved around Crispin Gantry, but she never thought of loving him . . . until her mother tried to end their friendship and Crispin told her bluntly that he looked upon her as a sister. Gemma was at the age to slip into love, to welcome the dawn of delight that was the first stirring of an adult emotion. She could not know that she offered her heart to the one man that she must not love . . .

JULIET GRAY

DAWN OF DELIGHT

Complete and Unabridged

ULVERSCROFT
Leicester

First published in Great Britain in 1967

First Large Print Edition
published March 1990

British Library CIP Data

Gray, Juliet, *1933*–
Dawn of delight.—Large print ed.—
Ulverscroft large print series: romance
I. Title
823′.914[F]

ISBN 0-7089-2154-X

Published by
F. A. Thorpe (Publishing) Ltd.
Anstey, Leicestershire
Set by Rowland Phototypesetting Ltd.
Bury St. Edmunds, Suffolk
Printed and bound in Great Britain by
T. J. Press (Padstow) Ltd., Padstow, Cornwall

1

"YOU'LL have to do something about it, Philip!" The vehement words were spoken by a slender woman in her early forties, still beautiful, still elegant and faintly arrogant in her calm assumption that she had only to command and people would leap to do her bidding.

Philip Gantry neither leaped nor trembled at her peremptory tone. He settled himself more comfortably in his deep armchair and continued to fill his pipe in the leisurely lazy way that always irritated Leonie Gardner.

Her hands clenched in the effort to quieten the sparking of her quick temper. She had tensed herself for this meeting, anticipating his lack of co-operation, his lack of realisation of the importance of her demands.

"Well?" she prompted as he remained silent, studying her with a faintly mocking smile about his lips.

"I really don't see what can be done, my dear Leonie," he said mildly. "Crispin isn't a child any more—the days when I could dictate his behaviour and his friendships are long past."

She knocked ash from her cigarette in a brisk, impatient, faintly querulous movement. "Well, Gemma *is* a child—or very little more. Just the age to imagine herself in love . . . and Crispin is much too attractive and far too attentive for my liking."

"He is an attractive young devil," he agreed carelessly as though he were not discussing his own son. "But I don't think you have real cause for anxiety . . . he isn't in the least inclined towards falling in love or thinking about marriage—or anything serious at all, you know. He's simply enjoying life in the way that one would expect from a boy of his age."

"I'm not worrying about Crispin—but about my daughter," she returned viciously, thrusting her cigarette into the ash-tray and grinding it to shreds. "You really are impossible, Philip," she added contemptuously. "You're taking this much too lightly . . . one would imagine that you don't realise what is involved!"

"I realise what you believe is involved," he returned smoothly. "But I think you're attaching too much importance to a boy-and-girl friendship."

"You haven't a daughter!" she snapped. "So you can't possibly judge the effect of an attractive young man's attentions on a romantic and impressionable girl."

He raised a quizzical eyebrow. "We are still talking about Gemma?"

Leonie glared at him. "Of course!"

"Impressionable? Where Crispin is concerned? Having known him since infancy, virtually grown up with him, played with him, fought with him and treated him much like an irritating brother for eighteen years! No, no, Leonie. . . Gemma can't possibly have any romantic illusions about Crispin and I don't believe that she cherishes any tender feeling for him." There was a hint of dry amusement in his tone.

"Obviously you are as lacking in perception as you are in understanding," she told him cuttingly. "You must allow me to know my own daughter."

"Well, what do you expect me to do?" he asked patiently, striking a match and applying the flame to the bowl of his pipe.

"Discourage a ridiculous and dangerous flirtation before it becomes something more," she retorted promptly.

Philip studied her for a long moment. Then he said quietly: "You may be a very intelligent woman—but you have very little ordinary common-sense. Young people thrive on opposition! Any attempt on my part to prevent Crispin from dancing attendance on your daughter would only drive him further into her arms—and particularly so if he feels nothing for her but the affection and friendship one would expect after all these years. They are good friends . . . they enjoy each other's company and have much in common. I'm quite convinced that Crispin's manner towards Gemma is that of a brother rather than a possible lover—and you must allow me to know my own son," he added with a humorous twinkle in his grey eyes.

Leonie stiffened with annoyance. "I should have known it would be a waste of time to talk to you! It has always been one of your greatest pleasures to oppose me, to thwart me if you can! It almost seems as though it would tickle your sense of humour if Crispin and Gemma fell in love —but you know equally as well as I do that such a disaster must be prevented at all costs. If you won't talk to Crispin then I must forbid Gemma to associate with him any more than common courtesy demands!"

"I think she would find it very difficult to obey you," he said drily. "We are near neighbours, we have kept up an unconventional friendship for twenty-odd years and Gemma is used to living in Crispin's pocket, so to speak. And I think you would soon find yourself with exactly the unfortunate complication that you wish to prevent—and which I agree can only bring a great deal of unhappiness on their heads. Don't meddle, Leonie—and for heaven's sake try to keep this business in its true perspective. Crispin is no more likely to wish to marry your girl than is Adam—or Balfour, for that matter!"

She threw him a withering look as, gathering up bag and gloves, she rose to her feet. "I have no wish to see Gemma married to any Gantry . . . but if she must then Adam or Balfour are a thousand times more eligible than Crispin." She walked towards the door and he rose without haste to follow her from the room and into the hall. She allowed him to open the door for her in an outraged silence and then she bade him a curt goodbye and moved towards her waiting car.

"Leonie . . ." She turned with a gesture of impatience as he called her name. "Does it ever occur to you to tell Gemma the truth?" he asked drily.

"Does Crispin know the truth?" she retorted tartly—but she could not throw the tall, lean, shrewd and level-headed man into confusion.

"Of course," he returned smoothly—and watched the mounting fury in her eyes and the hard, bright patches of angry colour leap to her cheeks.

"Then what the devil does he mean by being so much in Gemma's company?" she demanded harshly.

He gave a faint shrug. "He is fond of her, naturally—and it wouldn't occur to him that a girl who has known him all his life might suddenly develop a youthful infatuation for him. It seems that you're the only person to fear such a likelihood, Leonie." And, smiling, he nodded a courteous farewell and turned back into the house . . . much amused and not in the least surprised that Leonie Gardner, an open book to this man, should have made such a mountain out of a molehill . . .

His wife reached the foot of the wide staircase as he closed the heavy door behind him—and she went to him swiftly, enquiry in her eyes.

"What *did* she want, Philip?" she asked lightly, relief touching her expression as she noted the amusement in his eyes. "I could see that my presence was most unwelcome so I thought it wise to remove myself so that she could unburden her troubles." There was no love lost between Muriel Gantry and Leonie Gardner—but in the circumstances it would have been surprising if they had become friends. The only interest they had ever had in common was Philip . . . and Muriel despised the woman whole-heartedly. She fully understood why her husband should have chosen to remain on good terms with the Gardners but it had always been an effort for her to meet them with smiling equanimity. She would never forgive them for the injury they had inflicted on her beloved Philip—even though they had unwittingly served her well at the same time. She did not dislike Amory Gardner . . . merely thought him a fool and much to be pitied in his choice of a wife. But she had good reason to detest Leonie and as the feeling was mutual they exchanged very little more than the necessary civilities whenever they met.

Philip slipped an arm about her shoulders and smiled down at her tenderly, reassuringly. "It was nothing more than a storm in a tea-cup, as usual," he told her lightly but with a certain finality—and Muriel, recognising that tone, knew that it would be futile to question him further about his conversation with Leonie Gardner. "And speaking of tea-cups . . ." he added with a lift of his eyebrow.

Muriel glanced at her watch. "Yes, indeed—I must find out why the tray is so late."

"No need . . . I gave Martin the nod to

delay tea until our unwelcome visitor had taken herself off."

"Oh, Philip!" she protested, her innate observance of the common courtesies immediately outraged. "You should have offered her some tea—on an afternoon like this!"

He drew her into the comfortable, spacious sitting-room. "Yes, it is warm, isn't it," he agreed, not in the least chagrined. He kissed her cheek with careless affection and released her to seat himself in an armchair. "Where are the noble scions of the family this afternoon?" he asked lightly.

Muriel walked to the fireplace to press the bell before taking a chair opposite him. "I believe that Balfour is playing tennis at the Waverleys . . . Crispin was dressed for riding and might be anywhere in the county at this moment. Adam had an appointment with Prior to discuss the annual repairs." She leaned forward to pick up a magazine and began to riffle idly through the pages.

"Ah . . . putting me to shame, as usual," he said, grinning. "Where do they get their energy and application, I wonder?

Certainly not from my side of the family —the Gantrys have always been lazy, pleasure-loving, extravagant devils."

She looked up, a laugh in her eyes and touching her pretty mouth. "You can't say that they dislike pleasure or hold on to money, Philip—not one of them! And I strongly suspect that within a few years they will all be as lazy as you are!" She added warmly, in swift and loving contradiction: "Any way, I won't allow you to claim laziness, Philip! You are never idle —just unhurried in everything you do . . . and that certainly isn't a bad thing!"

"My darling, what *would* I do without you?" he demanded softly. "You are such a comfort to me . . . it does a man good to be frequently told that he hasn't a single fault in his make-up!"

Muriel chuckled, her eyes warm and indulgent with her love for him. "Husbands and children thrive and improve on praise," she told him teasingly.

He was suddenly serious as their eyes met. "My sons and I certainly have good cause to bless the day that you came to this house," he said quietly, earnestly. "I might have been an embittered and cynical old man—and the boys would have been well on the way to ruin without your love and good sense to guide them."

She flushed with pleasure, touched with emotion at the unexpected tribute . . . and Philip, watching the soft, pretty colour creeping into her cheeks, thought how young, how serene she looked despite her forty-five years—and how much he loved her. He could not resist comparing this kindly, good-natured, even-tempered and openly adoring woman with the cold, petulant, selfish woman who had so recently angered and disgusted him with her stupid fears for her young and bewitchingly lovely daughter. Had she really imagined that he would have kept Crispin in ignorance of the truth all these years—and was she really so foolish, so criminal as to imagine that she could keep the truth from Gemma indefinitely?

He recalled Leonie's expression as he turned to leave her . . . she had been appalled, infuriated, to discover that there were no secrets between Crispin and his father. She must also have been relieved of a natural dread, deep in her heart and mind, to realise that Crispin had never by word or glance or gesture betrayed any animosity towards her—and heaven knew he could not be blamed if he chose to treat her with contempt.

He wondered at her thoughts as she drove back to her home . . . and decided with justifiable cynicism that he need not doubt that each and every thought that passed through her mind would be tinged with her innate and ugly selfishness . . .

Muriel was denied the opportunity of replying as Martin entered the room with the tea-tray . . . and by the time he had leisurely closed the door behind him, the moment had passed. She would not have known quite what to say, in any case, for while she was entirely lacking in conceit she knew perfectly well that Philip had not exaggerated the case. Heaven knew he had been inclined to bitterness when she first came to the Manor Hall in answer to an advertisement for a housekeeper—and the two older boys had been allowed to run wild in the months that had elapsed since they knew a woman's kind but firm hand. Crispin had been a mere baby and in the care of an efficient if impersonal nurse—

and he had suffered the least even though he had lost his mother.

Muriel had taken in the situation at a glance—and kindly, tactfully but very definitely set about improving matters. Those first months had not been easy— and, to complicate matters, she had foolishly—or so it seemed at the time—fallen headlong in love with Philip Gantry. She knew that it had never occurred to him that she might care for him . . . she had known too that his proposal of marriage had been a matter of convenience rather than love and she had been too wise, too perceptive, too understanding to betray the way she felt about him when she agreed without emotion to become his wife. She had never ceased to marvel throughout the twenty years of their marriage that he should have come to love her so deeply . . . and she knew that she must be eternally grateful to him for the deep and lasting happiness that he had brought her. Her only regret was that she had never had a child of her own . . . but she had been busy enough with his three sons to have little time to dwell on her disappointment—and she had never needed to doubt that Philip shared her feeling of regret.

As he relaxed in his chair, his eyes closed, she studied him ... thinking how much she loved him, this kind, considerate, unselfish and courteous man she had married. He was a handsome man with his lean, bronzed good looks, the twinkling grey eyes and sensitive, humorous mouth, the crisp dark hair silvering now at the temples—how could she have helped but fall in love with him all those years ago ... and how incredible it still seemed that he should have chosen to marry her, whatever his motives. It must have seemed an odd marriage to his friends and acquaintances ... the wealthy, handsome Philip Gantry and the insignificant little dab of a housekeeper who was almost painfully conscientious about "keeping her place." Philip had not tried to deceive her and she had been content with the little he had offered—and happier than she had dared to suppose she would be as his wife. Even in her wildest dreams, she had never gone further than imagining that one day he might become tolerably fond of her—and yet he had grown to love her deeply.

Her own family had not hesitated to point out to her the pitfalls of marrying a man whose background was not only far superior to her own but contained two previous marriages, one ending with the death of his wife and the other in the divorce court. Muriel had cared as little for the objections of her family as she had for the talk that had circulated in the district . . . idle speculation and malicious rumours. She had been much too happy and too concerned with winning Philip's love to care for the opinion of those who sought to emphasise that she had "stepped out of her place" by marrying him. Perhaps she had—but neither of them had ever regretted it and she had brought Philip a great deal of happiness . . . and that had always been her main concern.

Philip opened his eyes unexpectedly and caught her reflective eyes upon him. He smiled reassuringly as though he was perfectly aware of her thoughts. "Best day's work you ever did, my dear," he said lightly.

She coloured faintly. "What, Philip?"

"Marrying me, of course . . . I hope you were thinking the same thing?"

"And supposing I wasn't?" she teased gently.

"I should probably remind you that a dutiful wife always shares her husband's opinions—and point out that it's part of her duties to refill his empty cup without being urged to do so."

She smiled and bent over the tea-tray, her deft hands readily complying with the light-hearted request.

He watched her in silence for a moment —and then said abruptly: "You know, it's odd that Leonie should turn out to be a protective tigress where that girl is concerned when she never gave a snap of her fingers for Crispin."

Muriel looked up quickly, eyes narrowing—but she passed him his tea without speaking.

He stirred it thoughtfully. "She seems to think that Gemma is falling in love with Crispin—likely, do you think?"

He shot the question at her. Muriel was a little taken aback. She understood that he hoped and expected her to laugh at the very idea . . . but Muriel was not so sure

16

that it could be dismissed as laughable. Gemma was at the age when it was very easy for a girl to imagine herself in love . . . and Crispin was a very attractive and personable young man.

"I hope not," she said quietly. "It would be quite disastrous."

"Oh, certainly—I agree with Leonie there." His mouth twisted with faint bitterness. "It must be the first time we've agreed on anything in over twenty years. But she claims that Crispin is encouraging the girl to love him—which is the last thing he is likely to do, in the circumstances."

"It's fortunate that he's aware of the circumstances," Muriel said quickly. "Gemma is really a lovely girl—quite enchanting. And she has always idolised Crispin. That kind of thing can't help but appeal to a man—and Crispin is very susceptible to flattery, Philip. If he hadn't been told. . . ." She broke off, remembering that it had been at her insistence that Philip eventually explained the facts to his youngest son—and that Philip had been very reluctant to unearth old history.

She had understood his feelings—but still she had insisted.

"Yes, yes . . . you were quite right," he said, a little impatiently for he had detested that necessary talk with Crispin and always felt, deep down, that Muriel had been wrong to insist that he should know the truth. "But you couldn't have known that anything like this might arise, my dear—I still wonder why you were so determined that he should know that Leonie Gardner is his mother."

She smiled soothingly. "Because she *is* his mother—and every man has the right to know the truth about his mother."

"He was brought up in the belief that she was dead," he reminded her sharply.

"And took to pitying himself because there was no one in the world who understood him as his own mother might have done had she lived," Muriel retorted swiftly. "Have you forgotten that painful phase because I certainly have not? Telling him the truth knocked that nonsense out of his head."

Philip smiled at her, a little mischievously. "And made him very thankful that Leonie had left him behind when she decided that she preferred Gardner to me —and made him realise that you were a much better mother than he deserved and that he'd behaved abominably towards you."

She looked down at her cup. "Well, it was rather a hurtful time, Philip."

"Of course it was—and we did the right thing. He's as fond of Gemma as we all are . . . but only a crass idiot would allow himself to get too fond of his own half-sister!"

2

"YOU'RE both looking very serious," Adam Gantry said lightly as he came into the room. "Am I too late for tea? Never mind, Muriel . . ." as she rose to press the bell. "I don't really want any . . . I've been wallowing in tea all afternoon—Prior can't add a list of figures without half a dozen cups to sustain him." He threw himself into an armchair, his long legs stretched out, and smiled from one to the other. "Am I to hear the bad news?"

"Bad news?" Muriel asked in surprise.

"Isn't there any? That's a relief. You both looked so anxious that I thought it must be the end of the world at least."

"We were discussing Crispin," Philip said slowly.

Adam raised a faintly quizzical eyebrow. "What has he done this time? Run off with one of the maids—or pawned the family silver—or merely wrecked his car for the umpteenth time?"

"Isn't he spending rather a lot of time with Gemma Gardner these days?"

"Is he? I wouldn't know . . . I never keep tabs on him. Any reason why he shouldn't?" he asked lazily.

"Her mother seems to think so," Philip said drily.

Adam grinned. "Her mother would like to wrap Gemma in cotton-wool and keep her in a locked room away from the impertinent eyes of every man who looks at her. She is that fiend of all fiends . . . an over-possessive mother who questions the poor girl on her every thought, feeling and movement. She will turn Gemma into a self-conscious, suspicious, spinsterish girl who'll find it hard to get any man to marry her—and sometimes I think that is exactly Leonie Gardner's intention."

"Surely not!" Muriel protested involuntarily.

Adam looked at her with faint indulgence for her lack of worldly wisdom. "But, my darling Muriel, you forget one thing . . . Gemma is all she has and she means to hold on to her."

"Amory . . . her husband . . ." Muriel's

voice trailed off at the amusement in his eyes.

"Tired of her years ago—and scarcely can bear to be in the same room with her for more than an hour. She alienated all her friends years ago—quarrelled with her family when she had the appalling bad taste to run off with Gardner—and there is only one person in the world apart from herself who really matters to her . . . and that's poor little Gemma who will have a hard time convincing herself that Mama does not always know best when Mama has been drilling the opposite into her since the day she was born."

"How can you know all that?" Muriel asked in bewilderment.

Adam shrugged. "Most of it is common knowledge—the rest is ordinary perception. Haven't you noticed that Gemma runs whenever Mama pulls the strings?"

"She's very young," Muriel said slowly. "You'll find that she has a mind of her own when it comes to important things."

Adam turned to his father. "Did Leonie come here to tell you to warn Crispin off her innocent little child?"

"Something like that," Philip agreed ruefully. "Did you see her?"

"Passed her car in the drive," he explained. "I knew she'd be up to mischief —but surely she can't imagine that Crispin has any evil intentions. The girl might be his sister . . . as indeed she is," he added in sudden recollection. "I meant that it wouldn't occur to him to even flirt with her!" He grinned again, that spirit of mischief lurking in his grey eyes. "Mama was horrified, of course—Crispin is tainted with the Gantry blood and has been brought up in this evil house so it follows that he must be capable of any enormity."

"In all fairness, I must say that Leonie had no idea that Crispin knew the true circumstances," Philip said quickly. "And, you know, as Muriel has just pointed out to me, it wouldn't have been so surprising if Crispin, unaware of the truth, decided that Gemma suited him better than any of the other girls he knows. They have always been very close friends."

"Then it's just as well he's grown up with the truth, isn't it?" Adam returned smoothly. "Not that I believe such a thing

23

could happen, anyway—Crispin isn't the type to settle for the known and familiar. One of these days he'll fall headlong in love with a girl he's never seen before—and be swept into marriage by the lure of the mystery and the unexpected."

"Which would be very hard on Gemma if she'd learned to care for him," Muriel said quietly.

Adam looked at her sharply. "You know, I suppose that is always possible. I doubt very much if Leonie will have sullied her innocent ears with a story that doesn't do her very much credit. And girls do seem to be attracted by my nauseating little brother." He smiled as he spoke—a smile that took the sting from the words and gave them a mocking humour. "What is to be done, I wonder? How can we save the beautiful Gemma from the possible consequences of her mother's stupid folly? How can we prevent her from falling in love with the handsome and dashing young man who is forbidden by the shared blood in their veins from reciprocating?" His smile widened. "Red-blooded melodrama, isn't it? Should I nobly throw myself into the arena as a sacrifice—and cut Crispin out while there is still time?"

Philip smiled drily. "I don't really think that will be necessary. A word in Crispin's ear should be quite sufficient."

"Certainly . . . but do you suggest he should enlighten Gemma as to his reasons for seeing less of her in the future? Considering they have lived in each other's pocket since infancy it occurs to me that she will certainly demand some kind of explanation."

"It should be easy enough for Crispin to impress on her that he has fallen quite heavily for another girl who demands every moment of his time," Muriel put in lightly. "We can only hope that she will take it as lightly as she has in the past— which she will do if her feeling for him is what it used to be . . . adoring but childlike."

Adam smiled at her with warm affection. "We can always rely on you to come up with a simple answer to any problem, Muriel. I must admit that that wouldn't have occurred to me."

"Not while you were busily constructing

a melodrama out of a very human situation, anyway," Muriel told him drily.

"Well, it has all the right ingredients," he retorted. "I wonder it hasn't occurred to any of us before . . . the lovely Gemma and the handsome half-brother virtually brought up together—tell me, how was that ever allowed to happen, anyway? What on earth possessed the Gardners to remain not only in the district but as our nearest neighbours—in the circumstances?"

"For one thing, Amory is one of my oldest and dearest friends—and we prided ourselves on being too civilised to allow the matter of Leonie's preference for him as a husband to interfere with that friendship," Philip told him. "And for another thing . . . oh, I don't know. Leonie had no maternal instinct where Crispin was concerned but she was convinced that I'd founder hopelessly on the seas of child-rearing and be forced to turn to her for advice . . . I might even have been persuaded to hand Crispin over to her although I had stipulated that if she insisted on a divorce she must forgo every claim to him. I don't think I was harsh," he added defensively although there was not a trace of criticism in the eyes or expressions of his listeners. "She loathed every minute of her pregnancy, made a great deal of fuss about a perfectly normal confinement and virtually ignored the child when he was born. Frankly, I felt that she was not fit to take care of him—and the readiness with which she agreed to my stipulation seemed to confirm it."

"She must have been pretty sick when she realised that she was carrying Gardner's child," Adam commented with faint satisfaction.

"So one might suppose—but she gave every impression of delight and has cosseted Gemma every day of her life," Philip replied quietly. "Perhaps that explains why I am still so bitter where Leonie is concerned . . . my child meant nothing to her and she is still a most unnatural mother where Crispin is concerned."

"Well, he isn't an ideal advertisement for a loving son," Adam retorted cynically. "He loathes Leonie and always has done so it has nothing to do with the fact that he found out in his teens that she had rejected him as a baby. And if he didn't know that Gemma was his half-sister and if it had occurred to him to fall in love with her, the mere thought of having Leonie Gardner for his mother-in-law would send him post-haste to the altar with someone else!" He glanced at Muriel who was smiling faintly at his emphatic announcement. "As far as Crispin is concerned, *Muriel* is his mother—and he loves her dearly . . . as we all do."

She looked at him, her smile deepening, her eyes warm with affection and misting slightly with the emotion evoked by his words. "Thank you, Adam—but that doesn't prevent any of you from plaguing me with your mischief and your scrapes from time to time," she said lightly.

"Oh, boys will be boys!" he retorted, grinning.

"For ever?" she teased.

"Yes . . . if they are lucky enough to marry someone like you," he told her, laughing. "Isn't that so, Dad?"

Philip was roused from the moody reverie into which he had fallen . . . and there was swift apology in the glance he sent his perceptive and understanding wife. The old bitterness had stirred in him —but that was unfair to Muriel who had done so much to eradicate it from his life . . . and after all if Leonie had not chosen to spend her life with Amory Gardner he would never have known the all-embracing happiness and comfort and peace of mind that had been his lot since Muriel married him. He would have continued to endure the hell that was his marriage to Leonie— and his sons would have grown up in a far from happy and satisfactory atmosphere. He had good reason to be thankful that things had turned out as they had . . . and surely he had sufficient compassion in his soul to be sorry for Leonie who had fallen blindly in love with a man incapable of response and equally incapable of refusing her desire to marry him. Amory Gardner had been bulldozed by a determined woman into a way of life that was alien to his nature and his desires—and he had rapidly retreated to his books and his writing and left Leonie to make the best of things with the little that he had to offer. It was not really so surprising that she should have become so fiercely maternal when Gemma was born—and because Amory took very little interest in his daughter and sometimes even needed to be reminded of her existence it was perfectly natural that the child's entire life had been influenced and dominated by her mother.

But Adam had turned to him with a question—and as he had not been following the conversation between his son and his wife, he turned a blank gaze to them.

"I was just telling Muriel that being married to her has kept you young, Dad," Adam explained.

He rose to the occasion adequately although he could not conceive how they could have arrived at that particular point. "Young—and superbly happy," he said warmly. "When you think of marriage . . . and I suppose we must eventually be rid of you . . . I hope you'll have enough sense to insist that your wife has all of Muriel's qualities."

"And none of my faults," Muriel said quickly, lightly.

Adam grimaced. "What an appalling bore she would turn out to be! You must allow her to have a few of your faults, Muriel dearest—perfection may be all very well for the connoisseur but I like my women to be human as well as beautiful."

"This conversation is bordering on the ridiculous," Muriel said, rising to her feet. "I have some letters to write so I'll leave you to entertain each other."

Both men rose and waited until the door had closed behind her before they resumed their seats. Such small courtesies came instinctively to them—and were much appreciated by the only woman in the family. She walked along the hall to the small sitting-room that was generally known as her sanctum—the room where she had received confessions and confidences from each of her adopted sons from time to time as they were growing up. Now the confessions were few and far apart . . . if they made mistakes, as they undoubtedly did, they were men enough to face the consequences alone and to deal with the ensuing problems without assistance from anyone. But Muriel was still their sympathetic and understanding confidante—and she cherished their affection and trust and was thankful that there were still times when they needed her despite the fact that they were all grown men.

She had tried not to favour one more than another throughout the years—but if she had a favourite it was certainly Adam even though Crispin had been a mere baby when she came to the Hall and was the more easily adopted as her own. Adam had been six at the time . . . a tall, sturdy little boy whose grey eyes assessed her steadily before his engaging smile betrayed that she was acceptable to him. He had possessed an odd dignity for a young child and the air of thoughtful reserve was more marked because Balfour, a year younger, was so obviously a happy-go-lucky extrovert who took everything in his stride and questioned nothing . . . a lovable, mischievous little boy who had yet failed to captivate Muriel's heart so completely and swiftly as his older brother.

The little boys had grown into men— but there was still that difference between the brothers. For all his flippancy, Adam was a mature, reserved and critical man who did not give his affections easily: Balfour was inclined to give too much of himself too soon with later regret, throwing himself at life with impulsive abandon while his brother apparently never took any step without first considering it carefully and dispassionately. Crispin had been something of a problem during adolescence—temperamental, over-sensitive, idealistic and utterly self-centred—but as he grew older he had steadied and seemed to strive to model himself on Adam rather than the livelier, more reckless and somewhat irresponsible Balfour.

Adam gave too much of his time and energy to estate affairs: Balfour successfully managed the home farm but divided his life between work and play; and Crispin was adept at wriggling out of work in order to enjoy himself although he would apply himself with short-lived enthusiasm to any task that Adam set for him about the estate.

Muriel loved them all dearly—they were fine, good-looking, confident young men, pleasant, well-mannered, thoroughly likeable . . . Adam and Balfour had the deep auburn hair of their mother and the twinkling grey eyes that were so like Philip's: Crispin, the handsome blond with the deep, laughing blue eyes—very much like his mother in colouring but with the clean-cut, slightly arrogant good looks that marked him as a Gantry.

Muriel sat down at the rosewood writing bureau, uncapped her fountain pen and drew the headed notepaper towards her. A letter to her widowed sister was long overdue . . . but she would temper her neglect with an invitation for Una and her daughter to spend some part of the summer at the Hall. She had discussed it with Philip and they had agreed that it would be good for Una to be dragged out of the mire of self-pity into which she seemed to have allowed herself to sink and that it would bring a little brightness into her daughter's life for Bess could not have had an easy time of it during the last few months. Muriel had little love for her sister who had made a bad marriage and never ceased to bemoan the fact—but she was fond of Bess and was already making plans for her entertainment during the summer months. She did not doubt that Una would accept the invitation with alacrity for while she had been the loudest objector at the time of Muriel's marriage to Philip she had long since acclaimed its many advantages and openly envied her sister and complimented her on her "cleverness" in catching such an elegible husband. Muriel detested the implications of her sister's changed attitude and would have severed the family tie years ago if Philip, so kind and compassionate, had not pointed out that Una was most unfortunate in her choice of a husband, knew a miserable life with him and probably gained some comfort from knowing that her only sister was both happy and secure in her marriage . . . and it was only the habitual note of complaint in her voice that gave her remarks an unintentional offensiveness. So Una, her husband and their only child had been invited to the Hall from time to time—and Muriel, guilty because she could not feel a sincere affection for her sister, had always made them welcome and set herself to ensure their entertainment . . . knowing at the outset that their stay would involve everyone in embarrassment and discomfort because Charles drank like a fish and was utterly objectionable, most bad-mannered, loud-mouthed and a mass of small conceits.

However, Charles was dead . . . and Una might well be a different person without her difficult husband at her elbow, ready to leap on her for every ill-expressed remark, eager to argue with anyone who gave him a lead and humiliating his wife a dozen times a day with obvious and outspoken comment. As he had left Una virtually penniless and with very few happy memories of the years they had shared, it was perhaps understandable that she should feel sorry for herself . . . and poor Bess would have known the brunt of that! She was a nice child with much of her mother's former vivacity and none of her father's brashness. She was popular with her adoptive cousins, a pleasant, good-natured, lively girl with a ready smile and a willingness to be pleased that endeared her to everyone. And, thinking with affection of her young and pretty niece, Muriel bent her head over her letter and urged her sister in warmer terms than she had intended to come to them for a long visit almost immediately . . .

3

THE girl and her restless mount made a striking tableau against the background of a clear blue sky—the slender girl in her olive-green habit and the clean, elegant lines of the white horse. For a moment she paused, reining her impatient mare, scanning the green and rolling panorama beneath her. Her keen eyes found what she sought . . . the movement of a rider heading in her direction—and a swift, sweet smile curved the lovely mouth.

She relaxed the rein and spurred her mare and headed across the high downs to meet him, her long hair whipped by the wind, her face flushed and her eyes bright with eager expectation.

Crispin Gantry checked his horse's speed and Noble dropped into a canter . . .the young man watched the girl's approach with smiling admiration. She was a reckless rider: it was always neck or nothing with Gemma—a little surprisingly when one considered how shy and uncertain of herself she could be when she was not astride a horse. But she could handle her mare with expert ease and it was a pleasure to watch their approach as they moved together in perfect symmetry.

She brought her horse to a halt, swinging round so that they were abreast, and smiled at him—flushed, a little breathless and aware again of that unaccountable feeling of shyness which touched her now whenever they met although until recently it would never have occurred to her that she had any reason to be shy in Crispin's company.

"Sorry I'm late," he said lightly. "I gave Noble his head and he took me miles out of my way. He needed a good gallop, though," he said, leaning to stroke the stallion's glossy neck.

Gemma nodded. "Oh, it doesn't matter," she assured him hastily. "I knew you'd come."

He dismounted with careless ease and turned to lift her down from the saddle. She was abruptly conscious of the strength in his hands as they circled her slim waist and the disturbing nearness of him as he swung her to the ground and held her momentarily, warmth in his smiling eyes, before he released her and dropped to the grass at her feet. "Sit down and enjoy the view," he commanded. "It's a perfect day . . . seems as though we might have a good summer this year. Though Adam will be worrying about the crops very soon if this dry spell keeps up." He grinned at her and brought out his cigarette case.

Gemma was silent while he smoked his cigarette, her gaze on the village nestling at the foot of the downs, her thoughts with the mother who would be justifiably angry if she knew that Crispin was her companion on this lovely afternoon.

Crispin looked at her curiously, wondering at her abstraction. "Did you get a scold yesterday?" he asked abruptly.

"Oh no!" she said quickly, too quickly.

He grimaced. "You should have allowed me to come in with you and explain," he said with faint rebuke in his tone.

Gemma shook her head. "It wouldn't have helped."

"Perhaps not," he agreed, knowing only too well that of recent weeks the very sight of him by Gemma's side brought a certain angry coldness to her mother's eyes. "You explained what had happened, of course."

"I don't think she quite believed that there was something wrong with the car that you couldn't put right," she said ruefully.

"I may be a very handy mechanic where cars are concerned but even I would hesitate to attempt to repair a broken axle," he said drily. "It was damned bad luck— and if Gary hadn't chanced to come along at the right moment you would have been much later home than you were. It's quite a long walk from Seaford!"

"I suppose any mother would have been anxious," she said, trying to be fair. "But she must have known that I couldn't come to any real harm . . . after all, she knew I was with you!"

His mouth twisted wryly. "Exactly so."

She looked at him quickly. "Oh, nonsense!"

"Forgetting that I'm a Gantry?"

Bewilderment touched her eyes. "But that's so silly."

"Is it? Would your mother have been so concerned if you'd been with Billy

Meddowes or Grant Sullavan and happened to be late home?"

Elbows on her knees, she cradled her chin in small, slender hands. "Well, we should have phoned," she said slowly.

"Agreed . . . but there wasn't a telephone box in sight or a house within easy reach and we were both fully occupied in wondering how we were going to get home at all," he reminded her lightly.

"Mother would have been just as cross if I'd been with Billy or Grant," she assured him. "It was quite natural that she should be worried, after all, Crispin—for all she knew there might have been an accident to the car."

He studied her small face. "Then why are you still troubled about it, Gemma? What did Mama have to say that makes you ill at ease with me this afternoon?"

Colour swept into her cheeks at the perceptive question. "Oh . . . it's just . . . well, the questions she asks," she admitted, knowing it would be futile to deny her sense of embarrassment.

Crispin frowned. "What kind of questions?" he asked sharply, fairly confident that he could make a good guess.

"Oh, the usual worried-mother questions," she said stiffly. She wrinkled her forehead in perplexity. "It's just . . . one would think that she doesn't trust you," she added uncertainly—and again the colour flamed in her young and very lovely face.

"I'm a man . . . with possible evil intentions?" he suggested lightly.

"But . . ." She glanced at him briefly, looked away again, discomfited by the mocking amusement in his eyes. "Billy Meddowes is a loathsome piece of work—paws every girl he can lay hands on. It's common knowledge—yet Mother talks as though she'd rather I ran around with Billy than you any day. She says that your reputation leaves much to be desired—and she would much prefer me to spend my time with a 'nice young man' and not risk my good name with you."

"I see," he said quietly, his mouth tight.

"It's so stupid! I've known you for ever!" she said, putting a tentative hand on his arm, afraid that she might have hurt him by impulsively repeating her mother's words.

"I expect Mama has her reasons," he

said lightly—but a familiar anger stirred that his parents should have made such a mess of their lives that this kind of situation could have arisen in the first place. He thought it incredibly short-sighted and stupid that Gemma should be kept in ignorance of the truth—and knew that it was far more than he dared to explain the facts to her although he had been frequently tempted to do so.

Gemma studied him a little shyly. "*Have* you a reputation, Crispin?"

He grinned. "Well . . . not quite as bad as Billy's I hope."

"You've never even tried to kiss me," she pointed out without a trace of coquetry.

Her naïvety amused him. "I should think not!" he replied lightly, privately thanking heaven that he had never known the slightest physical attraction for the bewitchingly lovely girl at his side. "I used to rock you in your cradle, my child," he reminded her with heavy pomposity. He rose to his feet. "Shall we ride to Bunty's for tea?" he suggested carelessly. "Challenge you to a race—and the loser pays!"

Gemma won the light-hearted race by a

43

mere length—and turned a glowing, triumphant face to him as he dismounted.

"I should have known better!" he exclaimed wryly, smiling up at her. But the smile did not touch his blue eyes. She was really enchanting, he thought soberly —no wonder Leonie Gardner was inclined to guard her too jealously.

Even though he had known Gemma since infancy, had grown up with her, took her looks very much for granted, he could still assess her beauty with the dispassionate, critical eyes of a stranger— and he was well aware that any stranger would catch his breath in incredulous admiration at first sight. For she was almost too lovely: long, waving mass of dark hair framing a perfect oval of a face with the truly violet eyes fringed by thick, dark lashes, incredibly long and sweeping her cheeks when she lowered them as she did so often in shyness rather than coquetry; the slender, shapely nose, the faint bloom of health and youth in her cheeks, the generous, warm mouth with its full, heart-catching underlip and the rounded, vulnerable chin . . . and as though the gods could not be too generous to this girl, a slender, perfectly-pro-portioned body that brought a hint of elegance to even the shabbiest of clothes.

So much loveliness could captivate a man even if he did not know, as Crispin Gantry did so well, that a warm, tender, loving heart, a sweet disposition, a ready intelligence and an appealing innocence of mind and spirit made her a delightful and refreshing person.

The dimple that lurked at the corner of her mouth vanished abruptly as her smile faded before his thoughtful gaze. There was such an odd expression in his blue eyes . . . an expression she could not analyse but which brought swift apprehension to her thoughts and feelings.

"Is something wrong?" she asked quietly.

Swiftly he banished his sober thoughts. "Not a thing," he told her lightly, lifted her down and drew her towards the farm-house where Bunty . . . Mrs. Bunter, formerly in service at the Hall and now supplementing her husband's income by providing the best farmhouse teas in the district . . . waited to greet them, beaming with pleasure.

"Now this is nice!" she exclaimed warmly as though they were not regular visitors but seldom-seen friends. "Taller than ever, Master Crispin . . . you've surely grown another inch—and Miss Gemma, pretty as a picture, I'm sure!" She smiled on them with romantic delight, thinking what an attractive pair they were and how nice it would be if they were to make a match of it one day.

She bustled away to get their teas . . . and Gemma lowered her long lashes to hide the amusement in her eyes. Crispin glanced at her suspiciously as that betraying dimple leaped to life. "What are you laughing at, infant?"

"Poor Bunty . . . she's always so disappointed!"

He smiled. "Is she? Why?" he asked absently.

She showed him her bare left hand. "No ring," she explained. "She always looks for it first thing."

He frowned. "An engagement ring, do you mean?" he demanded sharply.

"Of course! She's a terrible matchmaker . . . I expect she married us off when we were in our cradles," she said lightly.

He found his case and took out a cigarette with slow, deliberate care. "You imagine things," he said, a little curtly.

She glanced at him, surprised and a little puzzled. "Does it upset you?"

"Of course not! It's just a ridiculous fancy, Gemma . . . I don't suppose such a thing has ever occurred to Bunty—or anyone else!"

"I'm sorry," she said gently, realising too late that her careless words had been a mistake.

"Why on earth. . . ?" he said impatiently.

"I didn't mean to annoy you, Crispin . . . I know how unlikely it is—that it was a ridiculous thing to say," she said quickly.

"Unlikely? You mean impossible!" he snapped.

"Oh, I know . . . I mean—oh, don't be cross," she said shyly.

"I'm not cross," he said, his tone belying the denial.

"Yes, you are," she said gently.

He shrugged. "Well, of course I am," he admitted curtly. "You tell me that your mother doesn't think I'm to be trusted—

and then you try to flirt with me like any silly little girl. Who wouldn't be cross? I hope you haven't any stupid ideas in your head, Gemma . . . as far as I'm concerned you might be my sister and I never thought you'd need to be told such a thing!"

She was humiliated to the point of tears. She turned her head to stare through the open window, praying that he would not realise the unexpected wetness of her eyes.

Crispin looked at her small hands, unconsciously clenched, and immediately regretted his sharpness. He placed one of his strong, tanned hands over her clenched fists. "I'm sorry," he said generously. "I didn't mean to bite your head off, you know."

"It's all right." Her voice was muffled.

"Oh lord! You're not crying, are you?" he asked in horror.

"Of course not!" she returned with as much dignity as she could muster.

"Well, it looks suspiciously like it to me," he retorted. "What's the matter, Gemma? You never used to crumple at a bit of plain speaking."

Gemma fought the impulse to burst into

tears—and regained her composure with an effort. Growing up with the Gantry boys for companions, she had acquired a rather masculine contempt for tears and too much pride to admit to such a feminine indulgence.

It was all too ridiculous, she told herself with scorn . . . Crispin must have rated her a thousand times for various foolishnesses and she had never taken it to heart. Like him, she wondered what on earth was wrong with her . . . if these unexpected and unwelcome storms of emotion were all part and parcel of growing up then the sooner she reached maturity the better! After all, what had he said that could possibly hurt her so much? Hadn't she always known that he viewed her rather in the light of a young and often foolish sister?

She should not have mentioned her mother's strange distrust of him . . . she had been annoyed herself and scornful of the implication that Crispin Gantry could ever think of her as a woman instead of the "silly little girl" who merited no more than a brotherly, indulgent, companionable affection after all these years of having known each other. And it had never occurred to Gemma that Crispin might want to marry her one day . . . and, much as she loved him, she did not think that she would ever want to marry him.

Of course it was difficult not to feel possessive where Crispin was concerned . . . she had always thought of him as *her* friend, *her* property almost and she felt lonely and deserted whenever he neglected her for his latest flirt—and there had been plenty of those, heaven knew! But that was only because they were close friends and constant companions—and the days were long and empty and boring when she did not spend some part of them in his company. When she fell in love—and she supposed it must happen one day—she would be as thoughtless and neglectful of him as he was of her when another girl had prior claim on his time and attention. He had been in love half a dozen times but never sufficiently, it seemed, to want to marry any of the girls whose attraction for him had been so fierce and so fleeting. He called it "playing the field" and declared that he had no intention of marrying until he was well into his thirties . . . which comforted Gemma for she knew that once he married there would be no place for her in his life. What wife could understand the warm, intimate yet completely platonic friendship that existed between them? However, by the time he married it was very likely that Gemma would be married herself for it was possible, she supposed, that some man would come to mean as much to her as Crispin Gantry.

Having never been in love, she supposed that the feeling was very much the same as her feeling for Crispin—a warm, unself-conscious, easy and undemanding affection, a readiness to accept his careless and erratic demands on her friendship, the light-hearted, unthinking ease of conversation and the companionable silences, the slight ache of loneliness when she did not see him for days at a stretch and the surge of pleased thankfulness when they did meet. He was her dear friend: they understood each other—and if she sometimes resented the apparent ease with which he forgot all about her while enjoying himself with other girls . . . well, that did not mean that she was in love with him, she thought defiantly. She could be fond of Crispin without spoiling everything with silly, sentimental nonsense . . . and it would spoil everything! For didn't he always make it obvious that he thought of her as a sister? And didn't he rear like a startled horse if she thoughtlessly introduced the slightest note of sentiment into their friendship?

Which made it all the more ludicrous that her mother should have recently taken it into her head to warn her against Crispin and his attentions and to question her diligently and embarrassingly on his behaviour when she was with him. Gemma had all the vulnerable pride of youth and femininity and she disliked having to admit that he had never tried to kiss her and was more likely to offer light-hearted insults than endearments even though such information might reassure her unaccountably concerned mother . . .

"I have some news for you," Crispin said lightly, breaking into her thoughts. "Bess is coming to us for a few weeks."

Her face brightened. She liked and admired Bess Murray—and envied her very much. Bess was so gay and light-hearted, so very sure of herself, so much at ease in all situations and circumstances, so impulsive and friendly and attractive . . . It had never occurred to Gemma that the other girl might envy her for the sweet gentleness of her disposition, her quiet unassuming ways and patient acceptance, that appealing hint of shyness and modesty —and her long and easy association with the handsome Crispin and his brothers.

"On her own?" she asked.

Crispin grimaced ruefully. "No, unfortunately . . . but at least we are spared dear Uncle Charles. Perhaps Aunt Una will be less of a blight without him. . . anyway, Muriel will keep her occupied, I expect."

"When are they coming?"

"Beginning of the week. If the weather holds there'll be plenty of picnics and trips to the coast and swimming in the Tarn so keep your days free, won't you?" He grinned at her mischievously. "I suppose Mama won't object if she knows that you'll be one of a party instead of tête-à-tête with me?"

4

GEMMA ran lightly up the stone steps to the terrace, her face alight with the glow of pleasure in the afternoon and Crispin's company.

Leonie, relaxing in a chair on the terrace, straightened at her daughter's approach. She scanned Gemma's flushed face and noticed the sparkling eyes, the softly-curved mouth—and her own mouth tightened.

"No need to ask where you have been —or with whom," she said tartly. "Really, Gemma—aren't you a little old now for childish adoration?"

Gemma halted in dismay. "Hallo, Mother," she said lamely. "I thought you were out."

"Obviously. Or you might have schooled your expression more carefully." Leonie was taut with an anger that had its roots in fear and her obsessive love for this beautiful, dangerously innocent child. "I asked you only yesterday to spend less

54

time with Crispin Gantry—yet the moment I appear to be safely out of the way you rush off to meet him."

"We only went to Bunty's for tea," she said, her pleasure in the afternoon banished instantly.

"It doesn't really matter where you went, does it? What does matter is that you are becoming deceitful, Gemma— encouraged by that young man!"

"No!" she protested instinctively. "Why should you say so? Crispin hasn't an ounce of deceit in him—and I can't understand why you should turn against him so suddenly. What has he done, Mother? Why is it wrong for us to be friends— we've been friends all our lives and no one has frowned on it!" Her face was flushed as she challenged her mother and her heart pounded in her throat. For she had never dared to do so before—and scarcely knew how she dared now.

Leonie sent her a quelling glance. "Don't speak to me in that tone, Gemma. This is what comes of running wild with Crispin Gantry for a companion—and you ask me why I dislike it! He hasn't an ounce of respect or good manners—and you're beginning to follow his example!"

Those long lashes swept her cheeks as she looked down . . . but her lowered lids concealed resentment rather than regret for her rudeness.

"I have already asked you to see less of him . . . now I am telling you that you are not to accept any invitations from him without my permission. Is that quite understood? I won't have your name linked with Crispin Gantry—do you hear me? He is a disreputable young man and if you won't concern yourself with what people will say of you if you continue to live in his pocket, then I must put an end to the association!"

"Association?" Gemma stared at her mother in dismay. "We're *friends* . . . you mustn't make it seem so ugly, so dirty! Crispin isn't disreputable—and why should anyone say unpleasant things about our friendship? I couldn't stop being friends with Crispin—how could I, Mother? What possible reason could I give?"

"There is no need to give any. . . simply

tell him that I forbid you to associate with him," Leonie told her harshly.

Rebellion, stirring for the first time, loosened her tongue and stiffened her pride. "As if I could!" she exclaimed. "You surely can't want me to be so humiliated, Mother—and the Gantrys would think it so odd!"

Leonie raised an astonished eyebrow. "I'm not concerned with what the Gantrys might think, child. You will do as you're told—or go abroad to a good finishing school until you've forgotten this sentimental nonsense where Crispin Gantry is concerned!"

Gemma's eyes widened in surprised dismay. "Send me to school . . . Mother, I'm eighteen!"

"A very young and inexperienced eighteen with a head full of romantic rubbish," Leonie returned drily. "Louise Wakefield is your age and she is going to an excellent school in Lausanne for a year. It might be very good for you to accompany her, Gemma."

She dropped to her knees beside her mother's chair. "You can't mean it," she pleaded. "You wouldn't really send me to

Lausanne! I should be so miserable—and with Louise Wakefield . . . oh no! She's such a snob . . . so cold and unfriendly and supercilious—I've never liked her!"

Leonie looked down at the lovely, beseeching face—and realised with a tiny shock that she had never known Gemma to admit to dislike of anyone. With an effort she hardened her resolution to put as many miles as possible between Gemma and Crispin before her beautiful daughter lost her trusting heart to her handsome half-brother.

"Well, she has what you lack, child—worldly wisdom and self-possession. You're such a child that it worries me, Gemma—and like a child you're much too trusting and innocent."

Gemma sat back on her heels. "And that's wrong?" she asked with a catch in her voice.

"It's very foolish . . . particularly in your dealings with men," Leonie told her sharply.

"But . . . but I don't have any dealings with men," Gemma protested.

"Crispin Gantry is a man," her mother reminded her drily.

"Of course . . . but he's like a *brother!*" Gemma cried involuntarily.

Leonie winced. "Are you sure?" she asked quietly.

Gemma opened her mouth to utter emphatic assurance—and then, hesitating, closed it again. For she was a very honest girl—and she could not be unmistakably sure that her feeling for Crispin was not untouched by a warmth and tenderness that went beyond the affection of a sister for a brother.

That hesitation caught at Leonie's apprehensive heart—and her hands clenched abruptly and painfully as her long nails dug into her palms.

"Well, almost," Gemma said slowly. "I've never had a brother so I can't be truly sure . . . but he treats me just as I think he would treat a sister if he had one, Mother. You really shouldn't worry about Crispin and me—I wouldn't be so silly as to fall in love with him, you know. I'm not his type at all!" She smiled at her mother reassuringly. "Bess Murray is coming to stay with them next week . . . just wait and see how promptly Crispin will relegate me to the background and dance attendance on Bess! He's very fond of her, Mother—and he just takes me for granted and I don't mind in the least." She stifled the small protest of her conscience . . . it might not be strictly true but she had trained herself not to mind too much.

Leonie sighed softly, her resolution weakening. Now that she realised that Crispin was in possession of the truth, she knew that he would not be so foolish as to care too much for Gemma—and it certainly seemed as though her fears for her daughter's vulnerable heart might be groundless after all. The child was fond of Crispin, of course—that was quite natural. But she had plenty of sense and surely too much pride to allow herself to care for a man who openly showed that he did not consider her to be "his type".

Gemma slipped an arm about her neck, smiling, rubbing her cheek against her mother's smooth face, sensing that her annoyance was slipping away. "You will let me be friends with Crispin, won't you?" she pleaded. "His parents are your friends . . . how would you explain to them that you'd forbidden me to 'associate' with their son? And Crispin and I would meet at parties and picnics . . . and I couldn't pretend he didn't exist, could I, Mother? It would be uncomfortable for everyone—and you can't really dislike Crispin so much when you've known him since he was born!"

Leonie adored her daughter. How could she help but soften when the child nestled close, slipped an arm about her neck and raised such soft, beautiful, pleading eyes to her face? And she had to admit the logic of her arguments. Outwardly the Gardners and the Gantrys were friends . . . they were close neighbours and it was obviously impossible to be on bad terms. They had all considered themselves too civilised, too adult to treat each other as pariahs—and at the time it had seemed the height of desirable sophistication to present the world with an unconventional friendship. Much as she would prefer a complete break between Crispin and Gemma it was obviously out of the question—and would only give rise to a great deal of unwelcome gossip and speculation.

Her threat to send Gemma away had

been empty . . . it had occurred to her when she learned that Louise Wakefield was going to Lausanne. But she knew she could not carry it out . . . it had been painful enough during the years of Gemma's boarding school when the terms had seemed endless and the holidays— when she had seen little of Gemma anyway —all too brief.

Perhaps it was unreasonable but her fear that Gemma might fall in love with Crispin was very real. She had never welcomed the close friendship between her daughter and the Gantrys but it had been inevitable and innocent enough when she was a child. And it had never occurred to her then that Gemma might lose her heart to Crispin . . .the easy, almost-filial intimacy between them had seemed to argue the opposite.

But Gemma was eighteen . . . and the spring which brought her eighteenth birthday had brought a new bloom to her cheeks, a new sparkle to her eyes, a new awareness of life to a girl on the threshold of maturity. And it seemed to Leonie that her daughter's warm and constant affection for Crispin was the underlying cause of that bloom, that sparkle, that awareness. They were too much together—and there was a radiance in the girl's face and bearing when she was with him or had just left him that caused Leonie's heart to falter with horror. She wanted so much for Gemma . . . love and happiness and eventual marriage and the joys of children —and, like every mother, she feared heartbreak and frustration, hurt and humiliation, for her child and would do her utmost to avert these things.

It was right and natural that Gemma should fall in love—but not with Crispin . . . never with Crispin. For that was the path to heartbreak and frustration, pain and despair . . . and Leonie was not so devoid of maternal pride that she could not recognise how devastatingly easy it could be for any girl to love Crispin. He was handsome and intelligent, an engaging young man with a warm and attractive personality and a swift appeal for women. Deep in her heart, Leonie would rejoice for him when he fell in love, would wish him happy and watch the progress of his marriage with keen, almost jealous, certainly vaguely maternal interest—and, deep in her heart, she knew that he would never fall in love with Gemma even if the truth of their mutual blood had been unknown to him. For he had always taken her for granted, seemed blind to her youthful loveliness, had known her sweetness and appealing innocence too long to be truly aware of it—and he looked for vivacity and self-possession and sophistication in a woman, things that Gemma did not and might never possess.

Certainly it was not Crispin's part in this business that she feared . . . his attitude was so obviously that of an indulgent, affectionate brother—and she wondered if he had grown up in the knowledge that he was, in fact, her half-brother. He had never betrayed his awareness of the truth to Leonie, either by youthful sentiment or through instinctive revulsion against a cold, uncaring mother. He had always been courteous, respectful, at ease in her presence, treating her much like a courtesy aunt . . . and she could only admire him for it in retrospect.

But Gemma was young and impulsive and foolishly romantic—that love and marriage should evolve from a childhood friendship would have an enormous appeal to her . . . and it was inevitably Crispin she would cast in the rôle of lover. She had grown up with Adam and Balfour as much as Crispin, it was true—but they had grown into men while she was still a child and while the fondness remained it was understandable that they should still consider her a child and treat her as such for the most part. Leonie could have swallowed her instinctive protests. . . would still . . . if only Gemma's curious, stirring heart had turned to either Adam or Balfour. But Balfour was twenty-seven and naturally attracted to older women . . . and Adam, at twenty-eight, not only ten years older than Gemma but apparently little interested in women of any age and surely much too mature and serious-minded to appeal to a girl like Gemma anyway.

Leonie stroked her daughter's dark hair absently; she struggled with an emotional impulse to tell Gemma the truth *now* and make her realise how hopeless, impossible and fraught with danger it would be to allow herself to care too much for Crispin. But she valued her daughter's good opinion and love far too much to risk losing either or both—and Gemma was just at the age to recoil from a mother who had relinquished all claim to her son because she had fallen in love with a man who was not her husband. It would seem horrifying and unnatural and coldly callous to Gemma who would not understand now . . . though she might later . . . that the love of a woman for a man could far surpass the feeling she had for a child.

Leonie had never wanted children. Certainly she had never wanted Philip's child. She had realised the mistake of marrying him when she met Amory Gardner on his return from a lecture tour in America . . . she and Philip had been married just six months and Leonie was bored, bored, bored! She did not know why she should have fallen so deeply, so suddenly, so amazingly in love with Amory—but the realisation that she had done exactly that coincided with the discovery that she was expecting Philip's child. Bitter, frustrated, angry, she had resented the unborn child more because intuition assured her that Amory was equally in love with her. He was a conventional man—and Philip had been his friend for many years. Any other woman might have accepted the impossibility of a man like Amory Gardner allowing his emotions to over-rule the dictates of friendship . . . but Leonie had never admitted defeat in anything. As soon as the long ordeal of childbirth was over, she had handed Crispin to the care of an efficient nurse—and turned all her energies to the task of persuading Amory that nothing mattered—*nothing*—except that they should grasp the promise of happiness together with both hands.

Leonie had flattered herself that he loved her too much to allow friendship or convention to stand in the way . . . later she realised that he was weak and helpless in the face of her strength and determination. And Philip, apart from his insistence that Crispin was his son and remained with him and that she should give up all her rights to him, had agreed to an amicable divorce and virtually wished them happiness. Obviously because he had also realised that their marriage was a mistake . . . but while Leonie was thankful at the time that he raised no objections she had never quite forgiven him for being so blatantly eager to be rid of her.

Gemma had been born at a time when Leonie had finally and reluctantly admitted to herself that Amory had never really loved anyone but himself—and she had turned instinctively to the child for comfort and an undemanding, unquestioning love and need . . . the unfailing love she had sought in Amory—and sought in vain. Gemma became an obsession—and Amory was too much wrapped up in himself and his books to know or care that he was being pushed into the background by his own daughter.

There had been no more children and Leonie had been thankful. For Gemma must have all her love, all her attention, all her interest.

They had been happy years and Gemma had fulfilled all the tender hopes and dreams that had occupied her mother's thoughts when she was a baby: she was beautiful, she was intelligent—a loving, sensitive, delightful daughter. Now, abruptly it seemed, she was no longer a child but a young woman on the threshold of life—and love. It was not easy to accept that one day in the foreseeable future her beloved daughter would forsake her for a man she loved—but Leonie felt she could face that prospect when the time came. She could not face the thought of pain and unhappiness for Gemma . . .

She said carefully: "I don't dislike Crispin, darling. I just don't want you to be hurt, that's all." So swiftly had the thoughts raced through her mind that only the briefest pause had followed Gemma's wistful appeal.

Gemma looked up sharply. "And you think that Crispin means to hurt me? How?"

Leonie smiled—but she was careful to keep all hint of patronisation from that smile. "I'm sure he doesn't mean anything of the kind. But young men are inclined to be careless even with the best intentions in the world. You're so young . . . it would be easy for you to become very fond of him, I daresay. And easier still to imagine that because he falls back on you between flirtations he must be very fond of you."

Gemma again sat back on her heels and

stared at her mother in wide-eyed astonishment. "But he is!"

"Of course he is," Leonie agreed stifling an instinctive exasperation with her youthful innocence. "But not in the least in love with you, child—and I'm afraid you might be inclined to imagine that he is. That's possible, isn't it?"

Gemma was silent for a long moment. Surprise, dismay, embarrassment . . . her lovely face registered each expression in turn. "I don't know," she said slowly. "It hasn't occurred to me that Crispin might ever fall in love with *me* . . . why should he?"

Her sincerity and innate modesty were so blatant that Leonie cursed her own stupidity for implanting ideas into her head . . . and possibly her heart.

"Then I've been worrying about you for nothing," she forced herself to say lightly.

"Have you been worrying? Is that why you've been so strange about Crispin recently? Because I might be fancying that he was in love with me?" Gemma shook her head in abrupt negation. "I never thought of such a thing!" she exclaimed— a little too vehemently because only that day her thoughts had hovered on the brink of a vague question concerning her true feeling for Crispin Gantry. It was true that she had never imagined that he might love her—why should he? But she admitted for the first time that she had often toyed with the idea that she might be in love with him —if she could only be sure how one felt when one was in love! Perhaps she had always loved him . . . Juliet had loved Romeo when she was still a child, hadn't she? Certainly she often felt that no other man could ever mean as much to her as Crispin did—but did that imply that she loved him? Or was being in love a totally different feeling? She wished she knew— and wished her mother had not made her so supremely uncomfortable by crystallising a vague, undefined, almost breath-taking fancy . . .

"Then don't think about it again," Leonie said lightly, rising to her feet. "It's time you were dressing for dinner, child."

Gemma obediently followed her mother into the house in silence. Easy for her mother to dismiss the whole subject so lightly, she thought resentfully—didn't she realise the turmoil of her daughter's thoughts and emotions now that her admission of anxiety, her confession that she considered Gemma quite old enough to not only fall in love but to analyse her own feelings, had touched an innocent, valuable friendship with a self-conscious and unwelcome awareness of danger.

For it would be easy to love Crispin and she might so easily be in love with him now. But it was unlikely, she thought with a sudden stab of pain, that he would ever think of her as a possible candidate for his love . . . to him, she was just a little girl, lacking in the sophistication and sensual appeal of the girls who caught his fleeting but obviously desirable interest . . .

"Then I don't need to stop seeing him, after all, Mother?" she asked stiffly, pausing at the foot of the wide staircase.

Leonie hesitated. "My dear . . . I've no wish to interfere with your friendships," she said quietly. "And it would certainly be very difficult to prevent you from seeing any of the Gantrys—in the circumstances." She smiled at Gemma reassuringly—and wondered if she did not seem a little pale, a little tensed.

"They are our next door neighbours," Gemma agreed, forcing herself to speak lightly—and ran up the stairs to her room . . .

5

LEONIE went to her own room more slowly—and sat down at her dressing-table to repair her make-up. Gemma's parting words brought a wry smile to her mouth as she recalled them.

"Next door" was more a figure of speech than fact for the Hall was over a mile from the Manor House. But the Gantrys were their nearest neighbours, nonetheless—in that particular direction.

Philip had been born at the Hall—and his father and grandfather before him. Gantrys had owned much of the surrounding land for generations, tended it well and looked after their tenants and workers with loving and generous concern. Despite the demands of death duties, heavy taxation and the rising costs of estate expenses throughout the years, they were still one of the wealthiest families in the country.

In different circumstances, Leonie would have welcomed a match between her daughter and one of Philip Gantry's sons . . . preferably Adam, of course, for in due course he would have the lion's share of the estate and the Hall.

But she had rushed into marriage with a man she did not love purely for material considerations, borne him a son and gladly escaped from her marriage at the first opportunity—and while there was no legal barrier to a match between Gemma and Adam Gantry, Leonie recognised that it was not only unlikely but would be extremely unacceptable to her—and to Philip.

Looking back over the years while she skilfully applied lipstick and powder and tidied her blonde hair, Leonie thought without compassion how badly served Philip had been by his friendship with Amory. It had been his hand that brought Amory to the district in the first place. The death of the previous owner of the Manor had brought the property on to the market: Amory had chanced to mention in a letter to his friend that he was looking for a country house where he could write and study far from the demands of town life; and Philip had eagerly interested himself in bringing about Amory's purchase of the Manor House. He had obviously been glad of Amory's friendship and company during the years between Catherine's death and his subsequent remarriage—and he could not have foreseen that he was inviting trouble by his eagerness to have his old friend within throwing distance.

The marriage had been a dismal failure —and Leonie was honest enough with herself to admit that she had scarcely tried to make it a success. Philip had bored her from the outset: she had been selfish, petulant and terribly confident that she had him in the palm of her hand; when she realised that his love for her was as nonexistent as her love for him, that he had been swept into marriage through a combination of loneliness, physical desire and a vague concern for the motherless state of his sons, she had felt oddly cheated—and determined to revenge herself on him by seeking a man who would love her as she felt that she was entitled to be loved. She had not needed to seek very far . . . but it had never been part of her plan that she should fall heavily and astonishingly in love with Amory Gardner even though it had occurred to her that it might be amusing to sever a friendship which had always stirred a faint, surprising jealousy in her breast.

Who could have known or imagined that the quiet, studious, self-centred Amory could enchain Leonie with bonds of love so strong, so demanding, that husband, home and child could be summarily cast aside without a qualm or a single pang of regret?

It had all seemed so simple, so uncomplicated, to Leonie at the time . . . Philip would divorce her, she would marry Amory and they would sell the Manor House for a newer and much more convenient house at a far distance from Philip and the Hall.

But she had met with unexpected opposition. The divorce had been as straightforward as she could have wished—Philip had scarcely concealed his relief at the unexpected escape from a marriage that had become intolerable to him. Amory had been willing, if not exactly eager, to marry her—and Leonie had been forced to stifle the painful thought that he was prompted more by an out-dated chivalry than the kind of feeling that she had for him . . . a feeling that she had never quite been able to understand herself. She had been confident that she could manage Amory— and then she learned that the quiet, unassuming man could be surprisingly obstinate. He made it very clear that he had no intention of selling the Manor and leaving the district. He would not discuss such a proposal, consider her point of view or even agree that there was any necessity for such a step.

Living in a world of his own as he did, gossip did not affect him and he could not understand that it should distress Leonie: he valued his friendship with Philip and did not seem to consider it unconventional or eccentric to expect it to be unaffected by a domestic upheaval; he loved the Manor House and felt that his work was improved by its old and mellow atmosphere and for the first time in his life he felt that he had some "roots". His impending marriage to Leonie—still something of a shock to him—should not and would not involve him in further upheavals which could only affect his work on a new and very important book.

Leonie had accepted the inevitable. She loved Amory and she intended to marry him—and she was quite perceptive enough to appreciate that he might decide to cling to his comfortable bachelorhood if she made life uncomfortable for him at this stage. Her pride and her carefully-cultivated indifference to the opinions of others had carried her through the difficult time of gossip and disapproval and ostracisation. It had helped that Philip remained on friendly terms with them. If *he* could forgive and forget so easily, it was argued, then their neighbours in the district could do little but follow his example.

Life with Amory had not been easy. He had clung to his bachelor ways—and his self-sufficiency combined with the escapism provided by his work had made it very obvious to Leonie that marriage had made little impression on him. He was kind and courteous and considerate but he seemed so seldom to be fully aware of her as his wife—and she had only deceived herself that he loved her for the first few years. Then Gemma had been born—and it had no longer mattered so much that his books and his studies and his private world of historical facts meant more to Amory than the reality of his marriage to a lovely and desirable woman.

Gemma had compensated for more than Leonie had ever cared to admit to herself. She had filled an aching void in Leonie's life and eased the pain and humiliation of being overlooked and neglected by the man she still loved so desperately. For, against all rhyme or reason, she had continued to love Amory—and no other man had ever managed to stir her emotions one iota despite the loneliness and longing that her marriage had brought to her.

As Gemma grew up and reached adolescence, a dark shadow had touched Leonie's delight in her daughter—the fear that Gemma would inadvertently learn that her mother had once been Philip Gantry's wife, that she was the mother of Crispin Gantry, that she had deserted husband and child without a qualm in the selfish search for a happiness and fulfilment that had been denied her—perhaps as a punishment. Gemma was a loving and affectionate child, openly admiring and respecting her mother—but if she discovered the truth by accident how would she then view the mother who had devoted herself so completely to her since the day she was born?

The villagers had notoriously long memories . . . Leonie did not deceive herself that any of them were ignorant of the facts. But Gemma was so popular in the village, so pretty and appealing and so genuinely interested in the villagers and their humble affairs, that Leonie was sure that the dislike and disapproval with which they regarded her had never rubbed off on Gemma—and she felt that it was unlikely that anyone would dream of repeating ancient gossip about her mother in Gemma's hearing.

The Meddowes, the Sullavans, the Wakefields, the Barlows and the Kanes— the people who made up their "set", those who entertained or were entertained by the Gardners and the Gantrys . . . exposure was more likely in that quarter, Leonie had always felt. Not so much from her own contemporaries who would probably feel that it was either none of their business or else assume that Gemma had grown up with the knowledge of the truth —but the younger set . . . the young men and women who had either been mere children or not born at all at the time of the old scandal . . . those who would not know unless told by their parents that Gemma and Crispin were related by virtue of having had the same mother. How easily one of them might discover the fact through a chance and careless remark in their hearing—and how gladly that one would seize on an exciting bit of gossip and hurry to spread it among his friends!

But Leonie was no longer so aware of that dark shadow these days . . . Gemma was over eighteen and still in ignorance— and surely the young people, all growing up fast or already mature adults, would find little to interest them in ancient history of that kind . . . and perhaps, like their parents, would also assume that Gemma was fully aware of the truth.

How could she tell Gemma? Leonie demanded of her own reflection in the mirror. There was really no reason for her to be told, after all. Philip had assured her that Crispin had known the truth for years —and he had no reason to lie. Therefore it was even more unlikely that Crispin would ever regard Gemma in a romantic light—and she could scarcely be more fond of him if she knew of their relationship at this late date. If she did fancy herself in love with him—and Leonie still felt that it was only too possible—nothing could be gained by appalling her with the information that she was in love with her own half-brother. She would get over this youthful infatuation . . . it could scarcely be anything else and had probably only been brought about because Crispin was by far the most attractive and most appealing young man in the district. No doubt Gemma would fancy herself in love a dozen times before she finally met the man she would marry, Leonie thought comfortably—and it could only be a matter of time before Crispin met a girl he wished to marry and that would settle everything as far as Gemma was concerned . . .

She rose from the dressing-table, almost persuaded that all her recent anxiety and concern had been unnecessary—and even more determined that Gemma should never learn the truth from her lips . . .

She went to join Amory in a cocktail before dinner—and at that very moment Crispin handed a glass of sherry to Muriel with a smile.

She thanked him with a tender glance —and decided that he did look a little strained. She had half-convinced herself that it was only fancy . . . but now she realised that something was troubling him. It had never been her way to beat about the bush and so she came directly to the point: "You might just as well tell me now as later, Cris . . . what's on your mind?"

He grinned. "I'd never earn my living in the theatre, would I?"

"If you mean that you can't deceive me —well I've known and loved you a long time, my dear, and I like to think that you don't really have any secrets from me," she said lightly.

He threw himself into a chair and took a cigarette from the box on the low table by his side. Snapping his lighter into flame, he glanced up to meet the concern in her eyes that her tone had belied.

"Don't look anxious—I'm not in any trouble," he told her reassuringly. "It's just . . . oh, it's so damnably ridiculous!

Why on earth doesn't that wretched woman tell Gemma how matters stand? I nearly blurted out the truth myself today —and not for the first time."

Muriel sat down and regarded him thoughtfully, sipping her drink. She had learned long since that it did not pay to press Crispin for details . . . he was so like Philip in that respect.

He drew deeply on his cigarette, exhaled on a faint sigh of exasperation. "Perhaps her reluctance is natural . . . but Gemma isn't a child any more. And, frankly, I'm getting a little worried . . . Leonie's putting ideas into her head and I don't like it." He went on indignantly: "Why, she was trying to *flirt* with me today, Muriel . . . you can imagine how I felt!"

Muriel smiled faintly. "Oh, I expect she was only using you for practice, my dear . . .girls tend to do that kind of thing quite unconsciously at her age—and certainly without prompting from anyone." She sipped her cocktail, studying him over the rim of her glass. "But if it makes you uncomfortable then it might be wise to see less of Gemma for a little while . . ."

"Yes, I've thought of that for myself,"

he said, a little curtly. "But it seems hard on Gemma—and what would she think, poor kid?"

"Well . . . if you spend your time with another girl, she probably wouldn't think anything. After all, it has happened before, hasn't it?" she said gently.

"Agreed, but . . . oh, I don't know! Gemma's older now . . . she's growing up, she seems more vulnerable. I guess she takes me for granted a little—and that's partly my fault, I know. Whenever an affair with someone else ends, I rush back to Gemma . . . what girl could be blamed if she thought she had more importance in my life than the others, in those circumstances?"

"Why do you do it, Cris?" Muriel asked quietly.

He was taken aback by her question. "Why. . . ? Habit, I suppose—and because she didn't make any demands on me . . . something like that, anyway." He smiled suddenly, boyishly. "I guess she's good for my ego—and I've yet to meet another girl who's so willing to have her small world revolve around Crispin Gantry."

Muriel did not smile. She studied him thoughtfully and then said quietly: "Has it occurred to you that Gemma may be a little in love with you?"

He met her troubled eyes quite steadily. "This very afternoon. Is it surprising that I'm quite furious with Leonie?"

"Leonie Gardner is no doubt as anxious and dismayed by the possibility as you are, Cris."

"Then she should have told Gemma the truth years ago!"

"But she didn't . . . and you must appreciate that it would be very difficult for her to blurt out the facts at this late stage. Gemma is a sensitive girl and just at the age when she might easily turn against her mother. Quite frankly, I wouldn't welcome the task myself."

"She must be told," Crispin said stubbornly.

"Oh, I agree—of course she must be told. As soon as possible. Or she will find herself in the disastrous position of loving a man who has the same mother as herself. At the moment I imagine Gemma is a little in love with love itself . . . she's just the right age. Her romantic inclinations need to be turned in a different direction . . . and you can help there, Cris."

"What do I do . . . keep out of her way and hurt her by my neglect? That won't be easy, Muriel."

"It wouldn't do to be too abrupt about it," she pointed out sensibly. "You could avoid being alone with her, as a beginning . . . that should make it clear to Gemma that you need other people even if she feels that you're sufficient company for her. Bess will be here next week—and you'll be able to bring about party activities quite naturally. It won't seem odd if you are attentive to Bess—she will be a guest as well as someone that you don't see very often. Later . . . well, I don't need to advise you on the methods of paying court to other girls, my dear," she added lightly. "I'm not convinced by any means that Gemma *is* in love with you . . . I just think she might be on the verge of it and it would be a kindness on your part to avert matters now and save her a deal of heartache in the future."

Crispin nodded. "You're right—but does any girl fall in love without encouragement? I shouldn't need to assure you that there hasn't been any such encouragement."

"Of course not . . . but there might have been if you'd been kept in ignorance too," Muriel pointed out sagely. "She's a very nice child besides being quite exceptionally beautiful—or is your affection for her so brotherly that you hadn't noticed?" she added teasingly.

"Oh, I've noticed," he said grimly. "But I'm thankful to say that it's never disturbed me in the least—which surely proves the blood tie between us when you remember that I'm particularly susceptible to beautiful girls."

"But you knew of the blood tie," Muriel reminded him again. "If you hadn't it's possible that you might have been very much disturbed by Gemma's loveliness— and as Leonie can't be unaware that you are a very personable young man it appals me that she should have exposed Gemma to even the slightest risk of caring too much for you."

"The woman's a fool!" he snapped curtly.

Muriel sighed. "Yes, I'm afraid she is," she agreed quietly—and stifled the weak sentiment that the boy should not condemn his own mother in such round terms even if she had abandoned him at a very early age. Crispin owed her nothing . . . not love nor loyalty nor respect—and even as a friend of the family and a courtesy "aunt" during his childhood she had never won anything but faint dislike and contempt from her own son because she had been too absorbed in Gemma to have interest or affection or patience for any other child—and children were so swift to sense indifference in an adult.

Crispin smiled at her affectionately. "Oh, you don't like me to say so, nevertheless," he teased her lightly. "You are really much too kind-hearted, Muriel—but we wouldn't have you any different, you know."

He leaned forward to take her hands and lift them, one after the other, to his lips in a gesture that was wholly loving, wholly tender, wholly touched with respect and admiration for this woman who had stood in the place of his own mother and deserved every vestige of the filial feeling he felt for her . . .

6

GEMMA sat on the thick grass, careless of her white dress, her legs curled under her and smiled as she listened to the gay badinage of her companions. But there was a faint wistfulness in that smile that did not pass entirely unnoticed.

Adam, lying on the grass, soaking up the warm sunshine and enjoying the unaccustomed leisure, studied her with apparently lazy carelessness—and knew the sharp stab of compassion. He wondered if Crispin were not overplaying his hand . . . he seemed to be virtually ignoring Gemma in his slightly overdone attentiveness to Bess. And Gemma was always vulnerable where he was concerned although she was courageous enough to conceal her dismay.

She was never particularly talkative or vivacious, he knew. Therefore her willingness to listen rather than to take part in the easy repartee that was being bandied between Bess and Balfour and Crispin was not marked. It was rather odd that she was always taken so much for granted, he mused as he chewed on a long blade of grass and watched the varying expressions as they passed over her face. Perhaps it was because they had all known her since infancy and accepted her presence without question or surprise—or even very much interest, he realised with a tiny shock of surprise. That might only be applicable to himself, of course—she was a mere child and a man of twenty-eight took little notice of an eighteen year old girl.

But he was taking notice of her now—and for the first time it occurred to him that she was no longer a child. She had grown into a very beautiful young woman. Beauty did not stir Adam Gantry as swiftly and strongly as it stirred his young half-brother . . . but when it was allied to a quiet wistfulness and a shy reluctance to impress her presence too much on others he found it oddly disturbing . . .

Gemma sensed his gaze and turned her head as swiftly, as questioningly as though he had spoken. Their eyes met and he smiled . . . warmly, reassuringly—and she smiled a response that was all the sweeter for its faintly absent quality.

Why, she takes *me* for granted, Adam thought on a surprising surge of resentment—or was it only that his extra years made her even more shy of him, put him on a shelf where she would not dare to reach? The simile amused him even while he resented such a possibility. He was not quite in his dotage, after all—and many girls as young as Gemma if not younger had been known to betray awareness of his attraction for them.

Then he realised that her unawareness of him was merely due to her inability to be conscious of anyone but Crispin. Her thoughts, her glances, her affection and attention—all were concentrated on him who was uncomfortably aware of it and therefore striving too hard to appear unaffected. Yet her concentration was not really so obvious . . . naturally Crispin would sense it for he had always been the idol of her adoration, the pivot of her small world and it was only now that he had become truly conscious of it and disturbed by it. And Adam was conscious of that concentration because he was devoting his entire attention to the girl. He doubted that either Bess or Balfour had noticed that no one but Crispin existed for Gemma that afternoon—or sensed that she was hurt and bewildered by Crispin's rather blatant neglect. Bess would not know that he was used to paying a great deal of attention to the other girl . . . and Balfour was much too intent on vying with Crispin for Bess Murray's attention to notice anything.

Crispin leaned close to Bess to whisper something in her ear . . . and she nodded, laughing. And Adam watched the slow, soft colour steal into Gemma's cheeks—and he was abruptly aware of anger against the younger man. He understood Crispin's reasons and admired him for carrying out a difficult task . . . but surely the young idiot could be less heavy-handed. He was hurting the girl desperately—and surely only pride restrained her from making some excuse to leave. She smiled gamely as Bess turned to draw her into the conversation, even managed to make some light reply—and Adam saw Crispin turn away in slight confusion as Gemma looked at him fully, almost reproachfully, certainly with a faint, troubled question in her violet eyes.

He leaped to his feet, assuming a sudden burst of energy. "Long cool drinks all round, I think—and I'll volunteer to get them. Who'll give me a hand . . . Gemma, will you?"

She rose, brushing the shreds of grass from her skirt. "Of course I will," she agreed—and Adam wondered if she knew that she openly betrayed her thankfulness for the excuse to escape for a while from the constant jabbing of Crispin's open neglect.

He tucked her hand carelessly into his arm as they strolled towards the house. "You're looking very pretty today," he told her, smiling down at her warmly.

A flicker of surprise touched her violet eyes. Because she did not know what to say in reply to an unexpected compliment from a man who usually treated her very much like a baby sister, she said nothing —but she coloured once more in confusion.

He wanted to give her some words of comfort, some small reassurance—but he could scarcely tell her not to worry, that

Crispin was just like a child with a new toy and would be his usual, kind and attentive self towards her once the novelty wore off. For that would betray that he was aware of her feelings—and that would never do. And it would also be a lie. For much as Crispin might hate the necessity of slighting and hurting Gemma in this way, he did realise the necessity—and there was no kind way to discourage a girl from caring for him. He could not tell her why she must be discouraged . . . it was better to risk her contempt and cause her a little heartache and turn her thoughts to other men. Bess had arrived at an opportune moment—but if it had not been Bess it would have been another girl. And it was kinder to Gemma that it should be Bess—for she would understand that Crispin was bound to be attentive to a guest and a relative and the blow must be less than if he had neglected her cruelly for any other girl.

"I've enjoyed the afternoon," he said lightly. "It isn't often that I take a day off —and I did need the exercise. You play a very nice game of tennis, Gemma . . . has Cris been coaching you? My game is very rusty these days, I'm afraid . . . it isn't surprising that you knocked me into a cocked hat. I wish you might have done the same to Cris . . . he's getting a little conceited about his proficiency of late!"

"He gets a great deal of practice, I suppose," she said quietly. "We play together quite often . . . I think I must have picked up a few tips from him quite unconsciously. But he is a marvellous player, Adam—he does everything so well, I think."

"Except work—lazy young devil," he said lightly and without malice. "We're coming to the busy time of the year though . . .he'll have to pull his weight a bit more, I'm afraid. You may not see so much of him, Gemma—don't hold it against me, will you?"

"I don't expect to see much of him anyway for a while," she said, trying to smile easily and endeavouring to keep all trace of her hurt from her tone. "Naturally he'll want to spend some time with Bess while she's here—he's very fond of her, you know. He was really thrilled about her visit."

"They get on very well," he agreed carelessly—and stepped aside for her to precede him into the house.

He busied himself with the drinks and sent Gemma for ice . . . and while she was gone he took a cigarette from the box on the table. There was a very thoughtful look in his eyes.

The girl *was* in love with Crispin! He had treated Muriel's suggestion of such a thing with an easy lightness that was characteristic of him. But now he realised to the full the enormity of Leonie Gardner's deceit where Gemma was concerned. It was much too late to turn the girl's thoughts in another direction. She had fallen in love with his young half-brother—and she was doomed to a great deal of heartache. She was already suffering some pangs—and he was desperately sorry for the child. He knew what she must be going through. For Adam had not reached the mature age of twenty-eight without falling in love—and he had been unwise enough to fall in love with a married woman who, while willing enough to indulge in a little harmless flirtation, had no intention whatsoever of ruining a perfectly happy and secure marriage. He had recovered, of course—but it had been hellish while it lasted . . . and it had been poor compensation for all that suffering to realise at a later date that he had never really loved the woman in question, after all.

Poor Gemma. She was so young, so vulnerable, so ready to love and so eager to be loved in return. It was so fatally easy for a childlike adoration to grow into a more mature emotion . . . and there was no doubt that she had always considered the very ordinary Crispin to be a god among men. She had always blinded herself to his faults, his very human selfishness, his weakness which led him to drift with the tide rather than oppose it, his rather fickle nature and his easy assumption that if he did not mind a thing no one else would do so. He had never felt very deeply about anything in his life except his family . . . he could be casual to the extreme without even realising the hurtfulness of his attitude where other people were concerned. Look at the many times he had dropped Gemma like a hot brick whenever he was seized with a new infatuation . . . and then committed the crass idiocy of rushing back to her easy, undemanding company the moment the affair had ended! It was quite astonishing how immature he could be at times for all his pretence of sophistication, Adam thought with indulgent impatience. Any other man would realise the dangers of encouraging a girl to believe that she was of prior importance in his life even though he might stray occasionally to other fields. But either because Crispin lacked sufficient conceit or because he believed that Gemma knew, as he did, the truth of their relationship, he had never seemed to be aware of that danger.

Adam supposed it was inevitable that Gemma should have learned to love Crispin. He had been the axis of her small world for so long that it would certainly be difficult, to say the least, for her to think tenderly of any other man. And because the entire neighbourhood had been impressed with the fact that Gemma seemed to be Crispin's private property, no other man had attempted to draw her interest away from him . . . or perhaps they had attempted and been rebuffed because Gemma was "keeping herself free" for Crispin. Adam did not know the truth of it . . . he only knew that it was too late to avert disaster and he simply did not know how he or anyone else could prevent the child's heart being broken in the very near future.

It was possible to soften the blow of humiliation in the immediate present by attaching himself to her, by assuming a marked interest that he did not really feel —at least it would be some small comfort if she could feel that one of the Gantrys cared whether or not she was included in their social plans. It was scarcely kind to continue to throw her into Crispin's company—but it would be unforgivably cruel to thrust her from their thoughts and activities quite completely.

He was so deep in thought that he did not hear Gemma's light step as she came into the room. There was an air of anxiety about him that struck her quite forcibly— and because she was fond of Adam, having always admired him from the distance of the vast difference in their ages, she was immediately concerned. She placed the bowl of ice on the tray and went to him.

"What's wrong, Adam? Can I help?" she asked quickly, laying her hand on his arm.

He looked down at her absently for a brief moment, scarcely conscious of her. Then he realised the concern in the small, flower-like face that was upturned to him . . . and he swiftly clasped her hand with his own. He was not an impulsive man . . . he rarely spoke without thinking or made any move without careful consideration. But he followed an impulse then and said abruptly yet gently: "I'm worried about you, Gemma!"

She stared at him, the colour receding rapidly from her face. Without words, she knew exactly what he meant—and wondered that she had betrayed herself so visibly . . . and knew the sharp pang of humiliation at the thought that if Adam had seen and understood then so must everyone else.

He observed and understood the dismay and apprehension that shadowed her eyes. "No . . . they weren't watching you, Gemma," he said quietly with a hint of warm reassurance in his tone.

"And you were," she said, a little bitterly—and he was aware of an odd pang that she should resent his concern for her. But he knew how natural it was . . . one always hoped to successfully conceal the agonies of heartache and humiliation from the world.

"Yes—does it strike you as so odd? I've known you all your life . . . I think I know you rather well. Certainly I've always known that you've looked on Cris as a knight in shining armour instead of a very ordinary human being. You're growing up, Gemma . . . beginning to think of men —and one man in particular—as likely candidates for marriage. It's a very vulnerable stage in one's life . . . the dawn of delight that so easily turns to the dark of despair. Cris has spent a great deal of his time with you recently . . . I knew that Bess would take his thoughts and his attention from you—and I knew you were going to be hurt. I wish I could have prevented it . . . but there was nothing I could do, you know. And if I watched you today it was not prompted by idle curiosity and an unkind wish to witness your discomfiture, you know . . . I was concerned for you and I wanted to be ready to step in the moment I sensed that things were getting a little too much for you."

Gemma could not help but be conscious of the genuine kindness of his words—and she was vaguely astonished by the perception he had shown. Pain stabbed her anew as it occurred to her to wonder that he could have been so aware that she would be hurt by Crispin once Bess arrived on the scene—and yet Crispin himself not only did not realise it but almost seemed to have deliberately set out to inflict that hurt.

He read her thoughts with an ease that surprised her. "Don't blame Cris too much, Gemma," he said gently. "He's young and careless and lives only for the moment . . . he doesn't mean to hurt you. He's much too fond of you."

"But he doesn't love me," she said painfully. "And he never will . . . I might be his sister for all that I mean to him."

If only he dared to tell her that she was exactly that to Crispin . . . but he had no right to do so. "A man's sister usually means a great deal to him, Gemma," he said kindly. "It's poor consolation, I know —but you do have a very important place in his affections." He slipped an arm about her shoulders and smiled down at her lovely, despairing face. "You won't believe me just now, my dear—but one day you'll realise that while Cris is a charming young devil he'd make a hopeless husband and provider—and that you never really loved him at all. Eighteen is much too young for anyone to give their heart for all time, you know."

She wrenched herself from his embracing arm. "You must think I'm a child!" she said coldly.

He smiled ruefully. "No . . . I'm not so old as that, Gemma. Even if you do imagine that I have one foot in the grave."

"I don't know what you mean," she said coldly.

"Don't you? Never mind . . . the ice is melting and they'll think we've forgotten all about the drinks."

He moved to take the tray. Gemma hesitated, looked about the room with an appealing helplessness. Then she said hurriedly: "Will you make my excuses, Adam—explain that the sun has given me a headache? I can't go out there again . . . can't face them again."

He sent her a reproachful glance. "Gemma, don't disappoint me. I've been admiring your courage all day. Believe me, you haven't betrayed anything to anyone but me—and remember that I was looking for it! Do you want them to suspect that you're hurt by Cris's neglect of you—that you're a little jealous of Bess for being the object of his attentions?"

Her eyes were pleading. "Don't make me, Adam—please don't make me."

He gave a faint shrug. "Of course not. I wouldn't dream of persuading you to do anything that you don't wish to do." He managed to convey a faint regret and disappointment very skilfully—and knew by the way her small, slight body stiffened that he had challenged her pride. "I'll explain that you didn't feel too well—that the sun has been too much for you. . . and tell them not to expect you this evening."

"You've forgotten the ice," she said quietly, picked up the bowl and prepared to follow him from the room.

He smiled at her over his shoulder. "Good girl!" he commended . . . and Gemma felt that no matter what agony lay in store for her she could not fail his obvious confidence in her courage and self-respect and sense of pride . . .

7

GEMMA studied her reflection in the mirror. She was a little pale but that was all. She had expected to look completely different but only that faint pallor betrayed how much she had suffered that day.

Oh, Crispin had neglected her in the past, openly flouted his latest flirts, shamelessly scurried back to her when he was temporarily at a loss for better company . . . but she had accepted it all without question and never reproached him either by word or glance or attitude.

But the past had not carried this new awareness of a strange and difficult and disturbing emotion . . . in the past she had not been in love with Crispin Gantry. And now she was . . . quite hopelessly and helplessly in love with him. She had finally admitted the truth to herself that very day. And he had chosen to devote all his energy and interest and attention to Bess Murray— and she had scarcely existed at all for him.

At first she had been puzzled that a man so invariably kind and courteous should have been so offhand towards her . . . then she had been vaguely annoyed and almost ready to challenge him with his rudeness . . . and then she had been engulfed by a pain so fierce, so all consuming that there had been no room for bewilderment or anger. It had taken all her strength of mind to keep a smile about her lips, the truth from her eyes—and to prevent herself from attacking Bess with tooth and nail. She had been shocked by that last savage, instinctive impulse—shocked and dismayed and very much frightened for she had always liked and admired Bess Murray who was so self-assured, so gay and vivacious, so likeable and friendly and warm-hearted. It was her first experience of the ferocity of jealousy . . . and she had shrunk from the realisation of the emotion that had possessed her. And even as she realised that she was jealous of Bess, she realised the motive of her jealousy . . . and she had looked at Crispin with a new awareness of all that he had come to mean to her.

She loved him . . . she loved him

desperately, passionately . . . not with that lukewarm affection that was all that a child could give but with a fierce, blazing flame that carried her swiftly over the threshold of womanhood.

She had looked at him with new eyes . . . realising for the first time how remarkably handsome he was with his blond hair blazing in the bright sunshine and his very blue eyes seeming even bluer in his tanned face, the white even teeth gleaming as he talked and laughed with Bess who had never seemed more responsive to his attractive appeal than then . . . and Gemma had plunged into the very depths of despair as she knew that it would take a miracle at the very least for Crispin Gantry to think of her as a woman who was not only beautiful but beloved.

She remembered abruptly something that Adam had said to her . . . dear Adam who only meant to be kind, whose very kindness and perception and sensitivity she had never completely gauged before that day. He had been talking of the vulnerability of youth, the ease with which one could slip into love at a certain stage in one's life . . . he had mentioned the dawn of delight that could turn so easily to the dark of despair. And now the words came back to her—and she was surprised anew at his complete understanding.

For so she had felt that very day. . . that this was the dawn of delight, the promise of paradise on earth, the hint of happiness to come. She loved Crispin—and surely he must come to an awareness of her love and an inevitable quickening of his own emotions. It seemed impossible that a love such as she felt could be ignored, spurned, rejected—and she had blazed with a confident belief in the certainty of delight and paradise and happiness to come.

Their eyes had met . . . and she had known no shyness, no reluctance, no necessity to conceal her love—and he had dropped his gaze and turned away with a faint stain of dull colour deepening the tan of his cheeks. And Gemma had known that it was a deliberate and determined rebuff . . . a pointed implication that he had no need of her love . . . a painful hint that the old intimacy, the easy cameraderie, the delightful companionship of the past had no place in the future. She had only herself to blame, of course. . . it had not occurred to her then that he would not welcome her love even if he was unable to respond to it. But she could not doubt that it had been a mistake to reveal the way she felt about him—for that brief moment of unspoken communion had destroyed for ever all that they had shared in the past. Not only was she denied his love . . . she would never again know the comfort and security of his friendship.

Outwardly their relationship would be unaltered. He would treat her with casual and careless affection, continue to take her very much for granted . . . but there would never again be the same feeling of affinity between them that had almost bordered on kinship. He would not deliberately seek her company. There would be no more days of riding on the Downs, no more trips to the coast, no more memories to be cherished of long conversations, revealed confidences, shared secrets and easy, happy laughter and mutual understanding.

She had lost her dearest friend . . . and all because she had committed the folly of falling in love with him. And she wondered miserably what there was about her that made it so impossible for Crispin to welcome her love for him, so impossible for him to consider her as a likely candidate for his love . . .

She did not know how she was going to get through the evening. She had promised Adam that she would keep the engagement . . .and she would keep that reluctant promise. But pain was already pressing on her heart at the contemplation of an evening spent in close proximity with the man she loved while he danced attendance on another woman and offered her nothing but the merest of courtesies.

She knew that Adam would support her —and she knew that she was going to be much in need of his support. She had courage . . . she had pride—but she was also a young girl and in love and it would not be easy to pretend indifference while Crispin paid her scant attention. She could not be angry with him . . . it was no man's fault if a woman gave her love without encouragement or if he was incapable of response. But she was angry with herself for being so foolish . . . hadn't she always been aware that he shrank from any hint of sentiment in their relationship and hadn't he only the other day told her frankly that it would be impossible for him to feel anything for her but a brotherly affection? With that warning echoing in her heart, she should have guarded against the easy and treacherous mistake of loving him! But love was like lightning—and struck where it would. She had not deliberately fallen in love with Crispin . . . she wished now that it was possible to fall out of love with as much ease as she had slipped all unconsciously into it.

How long had she loved him without realisation? Or was it more true that she had realised it for some time without admitting that the emotion he had awakened could be a mature and adult love?

She loved him so much . . . she would always love him. And she would have to say nothing and watch him fall in love eventually with another woman whom he would marry—and she would never be any more to him but the girl he had known all his life, the friend and companion of earlier days, the daughter of family friends . . .a girl who had some small place in his affections born of long association and habit. She would gradually come to mean even less to him—and while he would enjoy a way of life in which she could never play a part, her life would be empty and cold and lonely without the warmth and comfort and companionship she had known because of their close friendship in the past.

Adam had claimed that no one gave their hearts for ever at eighteen . . . but she knew that he was wrong. Adam might believe that she was a mere child wishing for the moon and believing her heart to be broken because it would remain forever out of reach . . . but she knew that he was wrong. She was not a child and she could never love anyone but Crispin. No other man could ever mean so much to her as Crispin. She had no interest in other men. She loved him and she would go on loving him . . . she wanted it that way, too, even though it was all so hopeless and so painful. There was no crime in loving . . . she did not intend to make it obvious, to make Crispin uncomfortable in any way— all she asked was to go on loving him and she did not care that he would never give her anything but a mild and friendly affection. It was enough . . . she would make it enough. She would be so careful . . . he would never again be embarrassed by the naked truth in her glance. Soon he would believe that he had only imagined the love and tenderness he had seen in her eyes— and she would encourage him to believe it.

Adam knew the truth . . . but Adam was kind and understanding and trust-worthy. He would not betray her in any way . . . more, he would willingly help her to appear unconcerned when Crispin danced attendance on other women, help her to appear no more than pleased and interested when he eventually fell in love and planned to marry.

She must take the first steps to guard herself against public humiliation that very evening. The Gantrys were giving a party and inviting a great many of their friends and neighbours—partly because they always enjoyed entertaining, partly so that Bess should be assured of plenty of social invitations during her stay at the Hall. It would be obvious to everyone that Crispin was devoting himself to Bess—and disregarding any claim that Gemma might be supposed to have on his attentions. For it was no secret that Crispin Gantry and Gemma Gardner were close friends and frequently in each other's company . . . and at previous parties he had always set out to ensure her enjoyment.

Gemma knew that she must not appear to be hurt or annoyed by his desertion, his preference for the gay and bewitching Bess . . . she must chatter and smile with apparent ease, encourage the attentions of other men with an assumed coquetry, throw herself with apparent light-heartedness into the spirit of the evening —no matter what it cost her. She could not bear to cause comment, to arouse sympathy, to know that speculation was rife about her feelings . . .

Therefore she was thankful that the emotional stress of the day had not left its mark on her—except for the lack of colour in her face and that could easily be remedied. She was wearing a new dress for the first time and she had taken pains with the stylish arrangement of her hair—and as she looked at herself, almost a stranger, she decided that at last she had cast off the last vestiges of childhood. Perhaps there was a difference about her, after all—if it was only that new awareness of adult emotion. It helped that she had piled her hair on top of her head instead of allowing it to fall loosely down her back—that gave her an added maturity. And the dress was more sophisticated than her usual taste . . . cut low to reveal the gentle swell of her firm young breasts and most of her slim, tanned shoulders and slender back, straight-skirted and long-sleeved and extremely elegant. It was the soft, creamy colour of a tea-rose . . . and while she had protested when her mother chose the dress with an eye to the increased social activities of the coming winter, the fact that at eighteen Gemma would begin to attract more notice than she had done in the past and the need to provide the child with a wide choice of escorts in the future in order to wean her away from Crispin Gantry's company, now Gemma felt that the dress suited her need to appear mature and sophisticated and attractive to other men.

The door of her bedroom opened abruptly and Leonie looked into the room. "Aren't you ready yet, child?" she asked impatiently. As Gemma turned to her, she narrowed her eyes and swept the girl from head to foot with a long, searching glance. Then she nodded. "Yes . . . very nice," she said carelessly . . . but her heart had faltered at the realisation that her young and appealingly lovely daughter was at last a beautiful and oddly mature young woman. She could not hope to prevent some man . . . even a dozen men . . . from falling in love with the enchanting girl— and she must face the likelihood that Gemma would marry within the space of the next few years. It would be so hard to surrender her with a light heart—but a mother outgrew her usefulness and a child outgrew its need for its mother. That was the law of nature . . . and Leonie would not deny her child the right to happiness in love and marriage and motherhood even if she could. It was every mother's hope that her child would know complete fulfilment in life . . . but Gemma was still very young and Leonie sent up a silent prayer that she would not wish to rush into marriage too soon.

As mother and daughter made their way down the wide staircase and out to the waiting car, Leonie was thankful that she had accepted the invitation to the party that night. Amory had made his excuses, as usual—and Leonie, still seething from that last meeting with Philip, had been torn between polite acceptance and cold refusal. She was aware that the invitation had been prompted by courtesy more than a genuine desire for her company and it would not be the first time that she had allowed Gemma to attend such affairs without her chaperonage. But she had been so troubled of late by the disturbing apprehension that a boy-and-girl friendship might have developed into something more on Gemma's part, at least, that she had decided that it might be wise to observe the couple together and ascertain whether or not Gemma had given Crispin Gantry a special place in her heart with all the foolish impetuosity of youth.

Gemma was lovelier than even her mother had realised she could be . . . and Leonie attributed it to a natural excitement, and adult hairstyle and a sophisticated dress. Even Crispin, aware of the relationship between them, might be a little disturbed by her new beauty . . . certainly other men must be immediately attracted for Leonie did not doubt that her daughter would overshadow every other girl present that night.

Gemma was silent during the short journey to the Hall . . . she was mentally girding her loins for the ordeal ahead of her and clinging to the thought that Adam had promised to support her through the evening.

Leonie brought the car to a standstill by the wide stone steps that led up to the front door of the Hall. Although dusk had not yet fallen, lights were blazing from every window and the strains of music reached their ears. The party was well under way even at this early hour.

"No need to wait for me, Gemma," she said briskly. "I'll park the car farther down the drive and join you in a few minutes." Suddenly she smiled warmly at her daughter. "I don't expect you to hang around my skirts all evening, darling. You're a big girl now and I can trust you to behave yourself. Naturally you'll want to be with people of your own age . . . and I expect Muriel will have arranged bridge for the old codgers like myself who are a little old for dancing. I mean to enjoy the evening in the way that suits me . . . and I want you to do the same."

"Yes, Mother," Gemma said dutifully—but she had scarcely heard a word of Leonie's assurances. For she felt sick with apprehension and the prospect of pain and humiliation that were waiting for her—and she wanted nothing more than to turn tail and run home and seek the sanctuary of her room.

Adam had been watching for the car for some considerable time—and he had been on the point of deciding that Gemma had lacked the necessary courage and stamina to face the evening. He had been conscious of disappointment that was not entirely due to a belated and perfectly understandable cowardice on her part.

Now he came down the steps to greet them smiling, affable, matter-of-fact. "There you are! Good evening, Mrs. Gardner . . . would you like me to park the car for you?"

Leonie shook her head. "No . . . thank you, Adam. Are we very late? The party seems to be in full swing."

"It's going very well," he agreed. "But there are still some guests who haven't arrived yet . . . I'll take Gemma into the house and give her a drink, shall I?"

With a murmur of assent, Leonie released the handbrake and the car glided away from the steps and down the drive. Adam escorted Gemma into the house with a seemingly casual hand at her elbow . . . and she was glad that she had been spared the necessity of making a solitary entrance.

Two big rooms on the ground floor had been thrown into one to accommodate the guests . . . a small orchestra was playing at the far end of the room which had been festooned with streamers and balloons. An adjoining room had been drawn into service as a buffet and bar and a local firm of caterers called upon to attend to the food and drinks for the guests. A smaller room across the hall had been laid out with card tables and all the necessary adjuncts for bridge and two or three games were already in progress. The terrace had been prettily illuminated by fairy lights and the windows which gave access to it were all standing open for it was a warm night. The Gantrys were experienced party-givers and liked to ensure the complete enjoyment of all their guests.

There was no sign of Crispin as Gemma entered the ballroom on Adam's arm—and although she was conscious of a faint relief nevertheless she scanned the crowd with anxious, disappointed concern.

Adam pressed her slender fingers. "He's about somewhere," he said, reading her mind with that uncanny perception. "He was dancing just now . . . come along, I promised you a drink. What will you have?"

Gemma allowed him to guide her through the crowd to the bar, suddenly aware that she was causing a mild sensation. While she was faintly embarrassed she was also a little flattered. . . catching a few words of favourable comment as they pushed their way through a small group near the bar, colour suddenly stormed into her face.

Adam looked down at her and smiled, having also heard the words. "He's right, you know . . . you are stunning," he said quietly.

"Please . . . don't!" she protested, her innate shyness flooding her at his support of the compliment.

He turned to the bar, attracted the

attention of a waiter and procured drinks for them both. Gemma stood waiting for him, conscious that eyes were upon her, desperately striving for self-possession and a supreme acceptance of this unwanted admiration. Intently she watched the dancing couples in the other room—and all unconsciously her foot tapped in rhythm to the lively music of a quickstep.

"It is Gemma Gardner, isn't it?"

She turned swiftly to the man who had approached her. She had known Grant Sullavan all her life and she could not understand that faint hesitation in his tone.

"Don't be silly, Grant—you know me well enough!" she retorted—and was surprised that she was so successful in imparting a laughing coquetry to her words.

"But you look so different," he protested his genuine uncertainty. "Well, not exactly different . . . just older, I suppose. It's the hair-style, I guess."

"Quite likely," she agreed lightly.

"Come and dance," he suggested.

She hesitated. "Well . . ." She glanced over her shoulder. Adam seemed to be having some difficulty in extricating himself from a garrulous acquaintance—and he returned her glance with a faint lift of his eyebrow that indicatcd an apology for the delay.

Remembering her determination to impress upon everyone her indifference to Crispin's neglect by flirting inasmuch as she was capable of flirting with any man who looked twice at her, she capitulated with a smile and ready acceptance of Grant Sullavan's invitation . . .

8

IT occurred to Adam on several
occasions that evening that, after all,
Gemma had not stood in any need of
his support. She was the centre of an
admiring group of men every time he
caught sight of her—and if she was not
enjoying the party then she was giving an
admirable impression of enjoyment. She
did not lack for dancing partners . . .
someone was always on hand to provide
her with a drink—she was laughing and
talking easily and Adam would be
surprised if she was human enough not to
resist the flattery of so much attention.

Time and again he had tried to reach
her side to claim a dance . . . but he was
irritatingly caught by friends or acquaintances every time and it did not please him
that he seemed to be as much in demand
as Gemma.

As a host, there were certain duties he
had to carry out . . . and he found himself
dancing with a succession of plain and

unsought girls, providing drinks for certain elderly friends of the family, making introductions at frequent request, guiding bridge fiends across the hall and settling them to their game, checking that the drive was not becoming too thick with parked cars and circulating as freely as he could among the many guests.

His father was happily playing snooker with friends: Muriel had been coerced into a game of bridge, not entirely against her will; and, as Adam had expected, much of the responsibility for ensuring the success of the evening had devolved on his shoulders. Balfour was intent on his own enjoyment of the party and it seemed that he had ceded his earlier interest in the vivacious and attractive Bess to Crispin who scarcely left the girl's side all evening. Whether he was really becoming emotionally involved with Bess or whether he was going to extraordinary lengths to acquaint Gemma with his lack of interest in her as a woman, Adam could not be sure. And he was not so convinced of the lasting quality or depth of emotion in Gemma's feeling for Crispin that he did not hope that her success with the opposite sex this evening might turn her thoughts and affections away from Crispin, even slightly.

He had been as astonished as everyone else by her remarkable beauty which had seemed to blazon itself on the notice so unexpectedly when she arrived at the Hall. He had always appreciated that she was blessed with an appealing loveliness . . . but it had always been the immature charm of a child which impressed itself on him. Suddenly she was no longer a child . . . and whether that was due to the impact of an adult emotion on her personality or to the new sophistication of her appearance, he did not know.

He did not doubt that she fancied herself in love with Crispin. It was so easy at her age . . . and he could not deny that the younger man had a remarkable attraction for women. He only hoped that it was a passing fancy—and that she would be sensible enough to realise Crispin's lack of anything but mild affection and shake herself out of it. There was plenty of time for Gemma to fall in love in earnest . . . and she was the type of girl who needed a mature, level-headed, responsible man to take care of her—not an impetuous, reckless, careless, selfish young idiot like Crispin . . .

The impatiently-censured Crispin was struggling with an emotion that he recognised perfectly well as the onslaught of infatuation. It was a familiar emotion to him—but he had not expected himself to fall prey to it where Bess was concerned. He had always liked Bess, of course—who did not? But he had never visualised her as a partner in one of those light-hearted affairs that played so much a part in his life . . . until she had arrived at the Hall with her mother and greeted him with obvious warmth and an unmistakable sparkle of interest in her eyes.

She had always been a lively girl, brimming with merriment, a willing partner in any prank and blessed with an impish sense of humour to match his own. Now he realised the forceful attraction in her dancing eyes and the humorous curve of her lips, her husky voice with its hint of amusement—and he found himself stirred by a desire to hold her close and kiss those curving lips and know the sweet softness of her shapely body in his arms.

He had meant to devote himself to her

entertainment, in any case . . . conscious of the need to discourage Gemma from imagining herself not only in love with him but likely to be loved by him in return. But he had not expected to gain so much pleasure and satisfaction and stimulation from Bess's company . . . and while he had not intended to distress Gemma too much by his neglect he had found it virtually impossible to tear his attention from Bess for any length of time. He had sensed that Gemma was hurt but he had comforted himself with the thought that she was very young, that she could not seriously think herself in love with him, that she would accept his interest in Bess as easily and unselfishly as she had accepted his interest in other girls in the past once she had recovered from the initial dismay—and he had reminded himself that it was essential that Gemma should learn now that he was not her property and never would be . . . and perhaps she would begin to take an interest in other men and forget her romantic illusions where he was concerned . . .

He had been a little shaken when he caught sight of her that evening . . . and it was not surprising that his immediate thought was that she had set out to wean him from Bess by striving to make the most of her lovely face and figure. He was vaguely sorry for her but he realised that it would be a fatal mistake to gravitate to her side and allow her to think that she had made the expected conquest. Because Bess was such an entertaining and attractive companion, it was not difficult for him to restrain the impulse to bring Gemma over to join them. But he was a little uncomfortable, aware of a faint sense of guilt, knowing that his neglect and assumed indifference must be more than obvious to the poor girl . . . until he realised that she was so much in demand that she could scarcely be noticing his neglect at all, let alone being hurt by it. He told himself that it would have been her pride and not her heart that suffered at his hands if she had not been surrounded so rapidly by interested and attentive men . . . and he was glad that she was spared any humiliation she might otherwise have suffered.

He could not allow himself to believe that her heart rather than her pride was in danger. He did not dare to recall that moment when she had looked at him with a naked, rapturous flame in her eyes that had shocked him to the depths of his being. He had to cling desperately to the assurance that he had only imagined or else misunderstood that strangely tender glow . . .

He could not ignore her entirely throughout the evening, of course. . . whenever they caught sight of each other or passed in the course of a dance, he smiled or tossed her a casual, careless, light-hearted word—and only Crispin knew how difficult it was for him to appear light-hearted at those moments. He hated the faint heaviness of guilt that weighed on him, knowing as he did that not the slightest atom of blame could be laid at his door if Gemma had fallen in love with him —and yet aware that all unwittingly he had fostered her affection for him by maintaining the warm intimacy of close friendship for so long. It had never crossed his mind that she might become sentimental about him—until the other day. He had hoped that he had nipped such sentiment in the bud by his blunt warning—but was it possible that his immediate reaction had led him into a foolish mistake? She was young and undeniably lovely and just the right age to begin to expect admiration and attention from men . . . she might so easily have been piqued by his words— sufficiently to throw herself over the dangerous threshold of love . . . or imagined love . . . and determine to make him regret his words.

It was certainly odd that since Bess's arrival and the subsequent transference of his attentions, Gemma had contrived to make him unusually conscious of herself even while she withdrew into the background—odder still that she should have chosen this particular time to blossom into a new and mature beauty marked by elegance and sophistication. It was scarcely surprising that Crispin felt highly suspicious of her motives . . . and very reluctant to spend much time in her company . . .

Gemma was astonished by her sudden popularity—and vaguely suspicious of it. She could not help wondering if the men who flocked about her, mostly known to her by virtue of their friendship with

Crispin, had been prompted by him to entertain her. She did not doubt that if he had done such a thing then it was motivated by kindness, a desire that she should not seem to be ignored by him . . . but she was not so blinded by love that she did not know that there was also selfishness behind the action. Crispin had never enjoyed attacks of conscience—and surely his conscience must be active since Bess had arrived! For even Crispin, always so careless of her feelings, taking her complacence for granted where his many affairs were concerned, must realise that she was no longer a child, that she was entitled to a little of his consideration, that she must obviously be hurt by his abrupt preference for Bess. It puzzled her that he just did not seem to care, for while he might always have been irresponsible he had never before been cruel or indifferent . . .

And he knew she loved him! Of course he knew! No man could have been so unmoved, so unaware of all that she had allowed to show in her eyes that afternoon. She could appreciate that her love might be unwelcome to him even though she might fail to understand why he seemed to shrink from the very idea of being loved by her. But she could not accept that Crispin, her dear friend and companion for so long, would deliberately avoid her, deliberately set out to hurt her by a marked neglect—unless he had very good reason to do so.

How casual his smile, his light words, on the few occasions that they had come into actual contact during the evening! How obvious was the distance he kept between them! She might be a mere acquaintance instead of the girl he had known and loved like a sister ever since she had been in her cradle!

Oh, she did not lack for dancing partners, for male attention, for compliments and smooth propositions. But it was poor consolation when she ached to dance with Crispin, to laugh and talk with him in all the old intimacy of friendship and affection, to know the warmth of his hand clasping hers as they stood with a group of friends, to know that a certain smile in his blue eyes was intended only for her appreciation, to know that his enjoyment was only assured if she was happy and at ease.

She was too proud to seek out a man who would have so little to do with her— or to rebuff the men who gathered about her, urging her to dance, paying her extravagant compliments. She had never flirted in her life—but she flirted that evening with an ease that amazed her, handling the attentions of those men with an adroitness that she had imagined would be completely beyond her skill or self-possession. Her head was high, her eyes were bright, her laughter came often and easily, she was dancing beautifully—and she was conscious of a wild, triumphant elation that she was attractive to others even if Crispin Gantry considered her beneath his touch!

Gemma did not realise that the unusual amount of champagne she had been drinking accounted for a great deal of her high spirits. She did not know that the fever in her blood was due to champagne rather than the fierce urgency of a new, tender and vulnerable emotion that had swept into her life.

But Adam, conscious of a strange,

protective affection for her and striving to keep her under his eye as much as possible during that hectic evening, knew exactly what was happening . . . and knew exactly the right moment to desert his duties and take command of the situation.

He strode through the crowd to reach Gemma's side as she was laughingly trying to arbitrate a fierce argument between three would-be partners for the next dance. "I think I can settle the matter," he said smoothly, slipping a competent arm about her waist. "You promised me the supper dance, Gemma—remember?"

She looked up at him mistily. She recognised him, of course . . . but for the moment she simply couldn't put a name to that handsome, slightly concerned face.

"Did I? Oh dear!" She giggled. "I seem to have promised so many people all sorts of things."

"You may take my word for it," Adam told her firmly—and there was a note of steel in his voice that Gemma responded to exactly as he had expected.

"Of course . . . I do remember, Adam," she assured him. "I've been looking forward to it." And she slipped into his arms with an apologetic smile for her disappointed admirers.

Her head scarcely reached his shoulder and she was amazingly light in his arms. The faint perfume of her hair drifted into his nostrils. Perhaps it was the odd awareness of her that had troubled him all evening—or perhaps it was only that he was a man like any other. Whatever it was, he felt the desire to hold her closer than the steps of the dance demanded—and an even more disturbing impulse to touch his lips to the dark, coiled mass of her hair. Instead he swung her about the room with the expert ease of a practised dancer . . . and felt her steps falter.

"It's too fast . . . my head's going round . . . Adam, hold me—don't let me go!" The words tumbled from her lips in sudden panic.

His arm tightened about her obediently —and he thought how slender was her waist. He smiled down at her reassuringly —and thought how enchantingly lovely she was with those wide violet eyes and softly-parted lips and the faint flush in her cheeks. Skilfully he guided her through the swirling mass of dancers to one of the long, open windows and ushered her out to the terrace and the cool night air.

Gemma was grateful for the coolness on her hot face. But she had not realised that the sudden onslaught of fresh air would make her head swim again.

She clung to Adam, frightened. "What's wrong? I feel so ill . . . oh, Adam, I think I'm going to faint . . ."

He put an arm about her slim shoulders. "Of course you're not . . . you'll be all right in a few moments," he told her calmly. "It's only the fresh air—on top of all that champagne. Come and sit down." He urged her to a seat, made her sit down and then pushed her head between her knees in most unromantic fashion.

Gemma struggled for a moment . . . and then knew that the terrifying void which had opened before her was beginning to recede. Obediently she kept her head down—and gradually her full senses returned. Why, she was drunk! How awful . . . how humiliating! What must everyone think of her—and thank heavens her mother was playing bridge and perhaps need not know that she had almost disgraced herself in full view of half the county!

And Adam had known . . . Adam had come to her rescue. Oh, he was kind, thoughtful, considerate. And those beastly men had plied her with champagne, knowing that she was drinking too much and only concerned with the amusement she offered them by being unaware of it herself! How despicable! And how stupid of her! What would she have done if Adam hadn't seen, hadn't realised what was happening, hadn't come just in time and swept her out to the terrace!

She raised her head to thank him—and looked about her in bewilderment. She was alone! He had gone—probably disgusted with her folly and childishness! She could scarcely blame him. No man liked having to cope with a girl who had drunk too much and might so easily embarrass him at any moment. She only hoped that he had not gone for her mother!

Gemma buried her head in her hands . . . and slow, painful tears coursed down her cheeks. Adam had helped her—but it should have been Crispin. Crispin would have prevented those men from plying her with champagne, would have looked after her and warned her when he thought she'd had quite enough to drink . . . but Crispin had been much too busy to have time to notice what was happening. She wished she hadn't come to this beastly party!

"Here . . . drink this!" Adam spoke beside her, quietly yet peremptorily.

Gemma glanced up to see him standing over her with a cup in his hand. "What is it?" she asked stupidly.

He grinned. "Black coffee, my child . . . just what you need."

"Oh . . . thank you."

Adam sat down by her side and matter-of-factly took a handkerchief from his pocket and gave it to her. Gemma took it with a murmur of embarrassed thanks, mopped her cheeks, blew her nose force-fully and handed the handkerchief to him quite naturally. His smile deepened as he tucked it back into his pocket. "Now drink your coffee," he told her—and took out his cigarettes as she obediently sipped the steaming, strong liquid.

Gemma glanced at him shyly. "I'm making such a fool of myself, aren't I?"

"Are you?" he asked calmly. "I hadn't noticed."

"But you must think I'm awfully stupid," she persisted.

He looked down at her indulgently. "Do you want me to agree with you? Very well —it's bad policy to argue with a woman in your particular frame of mind."

She smiled . . . albeit reluctantly, it was still a smile. She had always known that he was kind . . . but his kindness had seemed so distant and avuncular where she was concerned. It was heart-warming to feel that the vast difference in their ages suddenly no longer seemed important . . . ten years was not so very much, after all. It was just that she had been still a child when he was a man with experience of the world. She was a woman now and while his attitude was indulgent and impersonal and only faintly tinged with affection, she did not feel that he regarded her as a child any longer. But she had no right to keep him from his friends, she suddenly realised—and said impulsively: "Thank you for the coffee . . . I'm all right now, truly I am. Please go back to the party."

Adam raised an eyebrow. "Don't you

care for my company, Gemma?" There was tender amusement in his tone.

"Of course . . . it isn't that . . . I mean . . ." She faltered and broke off, annoyed with herself for that stupid incoherency and for the embarrassment that lay behind it.

She fell silent, staring at the lighted windows, vaguely conscious of the sound of music and chatter and laughter—and yet feeling not the least desire to return to that crowded room. She was strangely content to sit with Adam and feel the strength and reassurance and comfort that seemed to emanate from his very presence . . .

9

ADAM touched her hand where it lay in her lap. "I assure you that the party is managing very well without me, child—I think I've devoted enough time and effort to it for one evening and I need the fresh air just as much as you do." He massaged his temples idly as he spoke, conscious of a vague tension—and wondering if it was only the party . . . or the strangely disturbing presence of the girl by his side.

"Do you have a headache?" Gemma asked in swift concern. "I have some aspirin . . . I'll go and get it and you can take it with some of my coffee."

He restrained her with a hand on her arm. "Thank you . . . but I won't need the aspirin. It isn't really a headache and the air will clear it. We'll just sit here for a while and talk or not talk as you wish, Gemma. How's your head now, by the way?" He smiled at her with warm understanding and solicitude.

"Oh, much better!" she assured him swiftly.

"And your *heart*," he wanted to ask—but he knew that a reassuring reply would not be forthcoming. For the moment she was more concerned about the state of her stomach and her head than she was about her heart—and he had no wish to remind her that she was supposed to be suffering all the pangs of unrequited love.

"I'm glad to hear it," he said lightly.

She turned to face him. "That was kind of you, Adam—thank you very much. I won't have any more champagne tonight, I promise . . . I *never* have more than two glasses, anyway. Crispin always says . . ." She broke off and then went on courageously: "He thinks that champagne is treacherous stuff . . . it seems so innocuous, just like lemonade, until one feels the kick in the back legs. Now I know exactly what he means."

Adam chuckled. "The kick in the back legs . . . yes, I can just hear Crispin saying it. I only wish he would always follow his own advice. Still, he's young—and he's inherited an excellent head from my father. I haven't, I'm afraid . . . I found myself under the table at a very early age and I've steered clear of the same position ever since. I'm a very cautious man, Gemma."

"Yes, I know," she agreed . . . and then coloured as he glanced at her with that amused tilt of his eyebrow. "I mean. . . Crispin is always telling me that you never do anything without considering it from all angles."

"It's a pity he doesn't do the same, sometimes," Adam said drily.

"He admires you tremendously," Gemma said quickly.

"And hasn't the faintest desire to emulate me," he retorted, smiling. "But I can't imagine why we should sit here talking about Crispin—there are a great variety of more interesting subjects in the world."

Gemma looked at him, widening her eyes. "Don't you like Crispin?" she asked naïvely.

"Of course . . . I'm very fond of him," he returned, a little stiffly. "But not blind to his faults, naturally. Knowing them doesn't mean that I either dislike or despise him . . . in fact, without them he wouldn't be such a personable and appealing young man. But we are still talking about Crispin—and he doesn't deserve so much of our attention. Tell me about you, Gemma . . . it seems incredible but I really know very little about you although I know so much about you."

"Isn't that a very cryptic remark?"

"Not really. I mean that I know all the trivial things—but I've never had a chance to find out anything about the actual Gemma."

"I suppose not," she murmured, aware again of that faint embarrassment. "You've always been . . . I mean, you're so much older . . . I guess you've always been so busy and I've just been growing up."

"I think I've already reminded you that, old as I may seem, I don't have one foot in the grave," he pointed out lightly. "I don't intend to repeat myself . . . just try to think of me as Adam—not ten-years-older-than-myself, much-above-me-and-terribly-experienced Adam. It really can't be so difficult as you imagine."

She laughed. It was only a whisper of a laugh—but it proved to Adam that the ready tears had been pushed back a little further.

"I don't know very much about you, either," she pointed out. "It's so easy to take people for granted when you've known them all your life."

"I've never understood why to be taken for granted is usually resented so much," Adam said quietly. "I think it's a popular way of considering someone to be reliable —and a reliable friend or relative can be very useful in life. And yet we do resent it . . . at least I do, I know."

"It can also mean having something . . . affection, friendship, even love . . . that you don't really value," Gemma said in a low voice. "Perhaps that's why most people resent it."

"Yes, of course," he agreed. "We all want our gifts to be valued and jealously guarded—and friendship and affection are particularly important gifts." He abruptly realised that they were still indirectly refer-ring to Crispin and the way she felt about him. "But we are being much too serious —and this is a party. Do you feel better? Would you like to dance?"

Gemma hesitated. During the easy

intimacy of those few moments, she had almost forgotten the painful episode which had led to this tête-à-tête with Adam Gantry. Now memory came flooding back and she did not know how to face the crowded room and the curious, amused, speculative eyes of those who must have witnessed her humiliation. Her only wish was to go home, to escape, to hope to forget the misery and heartache of the entire evening. She forgot that she had almost enjoyed the unusual attention that had been bestowed on her.

Adam smiled. "I hope you're not planning to run away," he said lightly. "Just as I can afford to relax and let the party manage itself—and spend a little time with you." He held out his hand to her. "Come along . . . there's a lot of the evening left and we can both enjoy it." He drew her to her feet and led her back into the house.

Despite Gemma's fears and convictions, no one had noticed those few moments of light-headedness or remarked on her absence from the big room. The supper interval had played too prominent a part in everyone's thoughts and the men who had been ousted from her side by Adam's quiet but firm appropriation had swiftly found consolation in other parts of the room.

Adam and Gemma slipped into the throng of dancers and although it took her some few minutes to raise her eyes to meet any glances that came her way and longer still to realise that no one was taking any interest in her at all, she soon relaxed in his arms and began to enjoy dancing with him. For he was really a very good dancer —and, a little surprisingly, much more human than she had supposed him to be. She had never expected any man as old as Adam to want to hold her just a little closer than the steps of the dance demanded . . . or to find that his cheek was firmly pressed against her hair. Not that he was old, of course—she smiled faintly to herself as she thought how swiftly he would refute the accusation if he could have read her thoughts. But she had never imagined that he could feel the least bit romantic about a girl of her age . . . or even about her! Yet there was something more than ordinary friendliness in the firmness of his embrace—and her heart almost stopped with the shock when he moved his head to brush her temple with his lips in what was unmistakably a kiss!

She looked up at him with astonishment in her eyes—and he smiled down at her warmly. "I think it's time we stopped taking each other for granted, Gemma," he said quietly. "Time we started to find out more about each other. Crispin has monopolised you for much too long."

The music ceased and he released her before she could make any reply. With a careless hand at her elbow he guided her towards a corner of the room—and Gemma went with him, unprotesting, too amazed by his sudden and surprising interest in her as a woman to think of anything else. It was not what she wanted, of course—it was impossible for her ever to think of Adam in a romantic light, in any light but that of friendship—and she racked her memory in sudden panic to wonder what she could have done or said to arouse his interest. It was all so puzzling. For, despite his easy words of a moment before, he was taking it for granted that she would respond to these strange overtures on his part . . . and yet he knew, had betrayed that he knew, how desperately involved her emotions were with Crispin. It simply did not make sense!

Balfour came across the room to join them. "My turn to dance with you, I think, Gemma," he said lightly. "I can't allow my brother to have things all his own way with the prettiest girl in the room." He grinned at Adam. "Don't you dare to object—or I'll tell her fond Mama that you've been out on the terrace in the moonlight for the past half-hour."

Before Adam or Gemma could say a word, he had swept her into his arms and away into the whirl of a quickstep.

Gemma looked up at him. "You shouldn't have said that, Balfour," she said quietly. "It wasn't what you think."

"I know that, sweetie," he assured her. "My sense of humour leads me into trouble all the time. I'm sorry if you were offended—and you know that I wouldn't dream of telling your mother if I'd caught you in a man's arms on the terrace. You're entitled to your little romances—and you're growing up very fast, aren't you? Faster than any of us realised, I think." He smiled at her gently.

But she scarcely heard his words for Crispin and Bess were passing them, dancing cheek to cheek . . . her eyes were closed and he was murmuring into her ear and they seemed to be absorbed in a wonderful world of their own. Painful jealousy stabbed her anew with frightening intensity . . . and she missed her step and trod on Balfour's foot.

He had followed her intent gaze and now he said quietly: "Don't take it too much to heart, Gemma . . . you know Cris . . . off with the old and on with the new in a flash. He doesn't mean to hurt anyone . . . he's just young enough to be hopelessly selfish and self-centred. He's playing a funny game tonight, though . . . I've never known him to be quite so offhand with you. No wonder Adam is putting himself out to look after you . . . if people talk at all it will only be about his unusual attentiveness to you when he seldom bothers with any girl at these affairs."

Gemma was spared the necessity of a reply when Adam touched his brother lightly on the shoulder. "Mind if I cut in . . . telephone for you, Balfour."

He hurried away and Gemma found

herself once more in Adam's strong and comforting embrace as they moved to the rhythm of the music. They danced in silence and Gemma digested Balfour's words with an odd little pang in the region of her heart.

Of course . . . Balfour was right. Adam was only being kind . . . looking after her! He had promised to do so, after all. How very stupid of her to imagine that it could possibly be anything else . . . that he could feel even the least little bit attracted to her. He was merely giving everybody something else to talk about—for it was well-known that Adam had little interest in women and did not flirt or play around as his brothers did. He scarcely even danced with a girl on these occasions . . . seemed quite content to busy himself with ensuring the enjoyment of others and the smooth running of the affair. It was certain to be commented upon . . . this unusual interest in the girl who was usually to be found with Crispin by her side—and people would be too busy speculating on the extent of his interest than to wonder that Crispin should have seemed almost indifferent to her presence at this particular party.

But Gemma did not want to be the subject of any discussion . . . and certainly she did not want Adam to be kind to the point of implying that there was a budding romance between them! He did not need to hold her so close . . . nor to kiss her hair . . . and she pulled herself away from him slightly. Immediately he loosed his hold.

"Something wrong?"

"I just don't want to dance any more," she said stiffly. "I . . . I have a headache. I wonder if Mother is ready to go home yet . . . would you excuse me, Adam. I must find Mother . . ."

He would not allow her to break away from him on the dance floor in full view of watching eyes. He took her hand and held it firmly in his own. "Your mother is still playing bridge, I expect . . . I'll take you to her, Gemma."

But Leonie was on a winning streak, had no intentions of leaving the game so early in the evening and was faintly impatient with the interruption.

"A headache . . . aspirins in my bag,

Gemma . . . take a couple and sit on the terrace for a few minutes. Fresh air does wonders for a headache."

"I'd rather go home," Gemma said hesitantly.

Leonie turned to look at her keenly. "I expect you've had too much champagne . . . you seemed to be having a wonderful time when I looked in before supper. Adam will look after you, child . . ." And she turned back to the game, studying her cards with a concentration that implied that she had completely dismissed the problem of Gemma and her headache for the time being.

Gemma sighed and followed Adam into the hall.

"I'll take you home," Adam said quietly.

Gemma shook her head. "I'd better wait for Mother." She sat down on the bottom step of the wide staircase. "I don't want to dance any more . . . it's so noisy in there."

Adam was puzzled by this sudden depression. "Did Balfour say something to upset you?" he asked gently.

A wave of misery swept over her. "Do you care?" she asked bitterly.

A faint smile touched his eyes . . . a smile of tenderness for the painful experiences of youth. He had not forgotten his own youth . . . the swift ecstacies and the rapid despairs, the imagined slights to a vulnerable pride, the painful awareness of all one's emotions and the ease with which one could be hurt. He remembered and understood and sympathised—and wondered with a faint stab of apprehension if this lovely girl, so young, so vulnerable, so appealing, could really be so much in love with Crispin. He had claimed so lightly that one did not fall deeply in love at eighteen . . . but was that true? Girls of eighteen did fall in love—even married.

"He always did talk too much—and say all the wrong things," he said lightly. "I should forget it, Gemma—whatever it was."

"It isn't just Balfour," she said impatiently. "You know what's wrong . . . I asked you if you cared? A stupid question! Why should you care? Why should any Gantry care about me or anyone else —you're all so damnably selfish and proud and wrapped up in your own little worlds. All of you—interested only in your own concerns. I hate you all! I wish I'd never known any of you . . . I wish I could go away and live somewhere where nobody's ever heard of the illustrious Gantrys!"

The words came tumbling out of that sheer black misery which possessed her . . . she had not meant to say those things but once they were said she felt no urge to retract them.

She was bitterly hurt and humiliated . . . perhaps more by the sudden realisation that Adam was only being kind to her than by any of Crispin's rejection and neglect. It was all too much . . . Crispin paying heavy court to another girl and ignoring her as though she had no right to his courtesy and consideration, no claim whatsoever on his friendship and affection . . . Balfour shattering her stupid illusions —and doing it deliberately, she was convinced, obviously aware that she could not help but feel a little flattered by Adam's attentions and believing them sincere . . . Adam being kind and gentle and thoughtful to the point of pretending an interest and attraction that he did not feel and which only humiliated her more because it could not possibly be genuine

—why should he bother with a girl so young and inexperienced who no doubt bored him to extinction except out of a misguided kindness—and, in any case, what right did he have to sense her feeling for Crispin and betray his knowledge and make everything so much worse! He must be lacking in sensitivity not to realise that no girl wanted to be told that she was wearing her heart on a sleeve!

Adam was staggered by her sudden outburst . . . he was also annoyed. He had the quick temper of the Gantrys even if he had learned to control it years before. "You needn't consider yourself so ill-used," he said coldly. "You've been as welcome in this house as a member of the family ever since you were born . . . and I'm damned sure that no one has ever treated you unkindly. I don't think you have any reason to hate us or to wish you'd never known us, Gemma—and I'm surprised that you should say such things. I know you're upset—but that doesn't excuse you. You're not a child any more . . . don't make childish declarations."

"Then don't treat me like a child!" she flared. "Tell me what's wrong with me

. . . what I've done! Is it so terrible that I should love Crispin . . . such a crime that he can't bear to have anything to do with me?"

He touched her arm gently with his hand. "I don't suppose Crispin knows that you love him . . . he is just head over heels where Bess is concerned and he doesn't realise that he's treating you badly."

She looked at him steadily, reproachfully—and he glanced away from that violet gaze. "It's deliberate—and you know it, Adam. I'm not a fool . . . I've known Crispin too long to be deceived. I only want to know *why!* Is it too much to ask that he could let me down gently—instead of treating me like a leper!"

Adam looked down at the glowing end of his cigarette. As Crispin had been so many times in the past, he was sorely tempted to tell her the truth and be done with it. But it concerned her mother too closely—and that was much too delicate a relationship to be threatened by disclosures of that kind.

"You're exaggerating Crispin's behaviour out of all proportion, Gemma," he said quietly.

161

Anger surged through her. She was convinced that he knew something. . . and was deliberately withholding it. She did not have the faintest conception of what it could be . . . but it did seem to Gemma that everyone knew something that she did not—and there is no more frustrating feeling than that!

"I suppose you believe that I'm exaggerating the way I feel about him, too?" she demanded furiously.

He sighed. "Don't force a quarrel on me, Gemma," he said wearily, wishing the whole damnable business was at an end. "I'm only trying to help you."

"Because you're sorry for me," she said bitterly on another wave of misery.

"Does that have to be my only reason?" he retorted, a little impatiently. "It isn't possible that I'm fond of you, I suppose— I've known you all your life, Gemma . . ."

"And I'm just like a sister to you!" she finished for him mockingly. "I've heard it all before—from Crispin. Ironic, isn't it? I love him—and he loves me . . . like a sister! I never thought I'd regret knowing you all so well—but I do!" She clasped her hands in a sudden onslaught of pain.

"I can name half a dozen girls you've known since childhood . . . but do you think of any of them as sisters? What about Bess? Is Crispin taking a brotherly interest in Bess? It's just an excuse for treating me as if I haven't any feelings—and it's a very poor excuse!" She leaped to her feet. "I'm going home—and you can tell Mother that I've gone!"

Before he could make any move, she had pushed past him and raced up the wide staircase to collect her things . . .

10

ADAM had every sympathy for her feelings but humanly he resented her attack on his family and felt faintly impatient with her dramatic display of emotion. He wished he had not allowed himself to get involved—it was not his problem, after all. Why the devil Leonie had found it necessary to make the whole thing into a dark mystery, he did not know —but in all fairness, she could have scarcely expected Gemma to fall in love with Crispin. He wondered a little sourly if Leonie knew what had happened—or if she was too self-centred to have any idea of what went on in her daughter's head or heart. Perhaps Gemma was more rebellious than he had supposed—for it seemed unlikely that Leonie would not have tried to interfere with Gemma's friendship with Crispin once she reached the dangerously romantic age of adolescence.

Crispin came into the hall and joined his

brother. He was slightly uncomfortable. "Where's Gemma?"

"I'm just about to take her home . . . she has a headache," Adam said non-committally.

Crispin stared at him. "Gemma? Not on your life, old man. I've never known such a thing. Upset, is she?"

"What did you expect?" Adam asked impatiently.

He grimaced. "I'm not very proud of myself, you know—but I didn't have much choice, did I?"

"There's such a thing as going to extremes," Adam said drily.

Crispin coloured. "I suppose so . . . but you know what women are. I had to make it as pointed as I could or Gemma would think that it's the usual kind of affair and I'd be dancing attendance on her again within the week. And you couldn't blame her either." He ran both hands through his hair. "It's a hell of a mess," he said unhappily. "Glad you stepped in earlier, Adam—I didn't like that crowd she was with and she was drinking too much champagne, you know."

"I'm surprised that you noticed," Adam said with heavy sarcasm.

"Well, you're in a foul mood, I must say," Crispin told him indignantly.

"Do you think I'm enjoying all this?" he retorted impatiently.

"No, I guess not." Crispin laid his hand on his brother's shoulder. "It's good of you to take care of Gemma . . . and I'm grateful. I know girls are not much in your line—and she is a bit young for you, anyway."

"Thanks," Adam said cuttingly. "I'm getting a little bored with being treated as though I were some years past my prime . . . I'm still some distance from thirty yet, you know."

Crispin grinned. "You know what I mean! She's only eighteen . . . just a kid, really. Too young to take anything very seriously thank heavens." He was suddenly sober again. "Poor Gemma . . . I feel rotten about the whole thing. Do you think I should talk to Leonie . . . tell her that it's time Gemma knew the truth?"

"No, I don't," Adam said sharply, knowing how impulsive Crispin could be and what trouble those impulses could lead him into from time to time. "Leonie wouldn't thank you for interfering . . . and she certainly wouldn't be pleased if you hinted that Gemma's getting too fond of you. Surely you don't want to make things any more difficult for the child?" He glanced towards the staircase. "She'll be down in a moment . . . you'd better go back to the party."

Crispin hesitated. "She's talked to you, I suppose, Adam. Did you get the impression that this is serious with her . . . it worries me, I'll admit. She's seemed different lately—been harping on engagements and that kind of thing. I had to be quite curt with her the other day—probably hurt her feelings."

Adam smiled at him reassuringly. "Don't worry, Cris . . . these things don't go very deep at eighteen. I shouldn't need to tell you that! I doubt if you'll ever be out of *your* depth with any woman!"

Crispin grinned. "Oh, I don't know . . ." He broke off abruptly as Gemma ran down the stairs with her wrap thrown about her shoulders. She paused as she caught sight of the two men . . . then she went on and would have passed them without word or sign if they had not moved towards her. She did not want to talk to Crispin—and, ashamed of her outburst, she did not want to face Adam again that night. But they left her no choice . . . and reluctantly she stopped.

"Going home so soon?" Crispin asked, smiling with affection and some concern and the faintest hint of apology.

"I've a headache . . . too much champagne, I expect," she returned as carelessly as she could. "Would you say my goodnights for me, Crispin . . . I don't feel like making the rounds."

"You do look a little pale," Crispin said in concern.

"Oh, I shall be all right," she said quickly, almost coolly, brushing aside his concern for her with the bitter thought that it was rather late for him to notice whether or not she was pale. "There's Bess . . .I expect she's looking for you, Crispin. Goodnight . . . see you soon." She turned to throw a quick, empty smile at Adam. "Goodnight, Adam."

Crispin looked at the older man swiftly. "But you're taking her home, aren't you? You said so!"

"Of course I am," Adam said, taking Gemma by the arm.

"There isn't any need . . . it isn't far and I can use the fresh air," Gemma protested.

"Nonsense!" Crispin said firmly. "You're not walking a mile on a dark night in those shoes, my girl—I'll take you home myself if Adam doesn't care to leave the party."

"You're not cutting me out at this late stage," Adam said lightly. "Go and dance with Bess—I'll look after Gemma." He smiled down at the girl by his side. "Come on . . . if your mother looks for you Crispin will tell her where you are."

He ushered her out of the house and down the steps. His car was in the garage and at his request she went with him to get it out for he suspected that she would slip away once his back was turned.

As they moved slowly down the drive, she sat beside him in silence, staring back at the house with its windows blazing with lights—and then she looked away and busied herself with drawing her wrap closer about her shoulders. Adam glanced at her. "Cold?"

"No, I'm fine."

He drove slowly for it was a lovely night and he did not think that she was really in a great hurry to be left alone with her thoughts and heartache—and that supposed headache. While he drove he talked to her, easily, desultorily . . . of people they knew, social events of past and future, the weather and things that their neighbours would get up while the sunshine lasted, riding and tennis and swimming. Her replies were brief and monosyllabic but he persevered.

Then Gemma said, abruptly, breaking into his words:. "Those things I said. . . I'm sorry. I didn't mean to hurt you."

He turned his head to smile, took one hand from the driving wheel to cover her clasped hands in brief reassurance. "I know . . . I'm not holding it against you."

The Manor House was in darkness but for one groundfloor window . . . a strange contrast to the big house they had so recently left.

"Father is still working," Gemma said without interest.

Adam nodded. "Do you want to go in . . . or shall we drive around for a while?

It's a beautiful night—and comparatively early."

Gemma gave a faint shrug. "I don't want to keep you from the party too long."

"I'm not particularly interested in the party—now," he said . . . and she looked at him quickly as he added that meaning word.

"Poor Adam," she said impulsively. "It's been a boring evening for you."

"Don't be silly," he said gently. "I only wish you could have enjoyed it—but I guess it was a mistake to press you to come."

Tears filled her eyes unexpectedly at the kindly warmth in his tone. She looked down at her clenched hands, suddenly too proud to have him know how she was feeling.

But Adam was strangely sensitive to her emotions. He turned to her swiftly, compassion stirring. "Gemma . . . you're so lovely. Too lovely to cry for a man who doesn't want you," he said urgently. "There are other men in the world, you know."

The tears that had threatened were shocked into submission by the quiet sincerity of his words. She sat very still, bewildered, a little apprehensive, uncertain of herself as he pushed a stray tendril of her hair behind her ear and then touched her cheek with the gentle fingers of affection. His hand moved to her shoulder and he bent his dark head until he found her cool, unresponsive lips. He brushed them only briefly with his own—and was astonished by the leaping desire to crush them into response with his kiss.

He had never realised the appeal that she could have for him . . . but now he found her overwhelmingly desirable. Her small, luminously lovely face was so very close to his own. But he knew that this was not merely physical attraction that stirred . . . it was a blend of desire and the wish to protect and a surging tenderness and a reluctance to rush his fences . . . and he wondered if he was falling in love with Gemma—and if he was capable of driving all thoughts of Crispin from her heart and mind. He could not want a woman who wanted another man . . . but how much did she want Crispin and how lasting, how true was the emotion that now possessed this young, unsophisticated and completely enchanting girl?

Gemma did not dare to speak or move. She was startled by the kiss that was not a kiss at all but hinted that it might so easily have been. She had almost allowed her lips to part beneath that provocative, fleeting touch . . . almost known the impulse to draw him closer so that the touch became a kiss. And she was shocked at herself! How could she even contemplate being kissed by someone else when she loved and wanted Crispin more than anything in the world? If the thought crossed her mind that she would have welcomed Adam's kiss, his arms about her, it would only be because she needed reassurance that she could attract a man . . . any man. And she would only have imagined that it was Crispin's arms that held her, Crispin's lips upon her own—and that would have been neither kind nor just to any man.

Adam straightened in his seat . . . and the simple movement broke the spell. Gemma turned to open the door. "I must go in . . ." she stammered.

He nodded. "Goodnight, Gemma."

"Goodnight—and thank you," she blurted—then she scrambled from the car and hurried towards the house without a backward glance.

Adam watched her, reaching for his cigarettes, surprised at the unexpected emotions she had stirred. What the devil was wrong with him? Could he really want a girl who was so naïve and inexperienced that she suffered agonies of embarrassment at the merest overture—and, more important, was in the throes of love, imaginary or otherwise, for someone else?

He watched her as she hurried across the gravel and mounted the steps. She rummaged in her bag for a key, opened the heavy door and closed it again behind her. She did not glance towards the car—and he was conscious of a vague disappointment. Yet he understood how startled—even apprehensive—she had been by his tentative approach. After all, she had probably never thought of him as an elegible man . . . he was just Adam, fast approaching thirty and having little interest in any women. It was something of a novelty and a relief for Adam who knew that almost every unattached woman in the county considered him a worthy prey and imagined he must eventually succumb to the lures that were constantly being thrown out to him. At the same time, he was chagrined by the evidence that Gemma thought him too old for her interest or for him to be interested in her . . .

He wondered at that interest on his part. Was it only compassion, an almost brotherly affection and concern? There had been nothing fraternal in his thoughts and feelings when his hand had moved from her hair to her cheek and down to that slim, firm shoulder, when he had sought her lips in that fleeting caress and known the soft perfume of her hair and skin disturbing his senses. It had required conscious effort to withdraw his hand, to move away from her . . . but he had sensed that to take matters further would have been a mistake. Whether or not she cared for Crispin, she was not the kind of girl to give her kisses lightly—and he did not want empty, meaningless kisses from Gemma. Without conceit, he knew that he was attractive to women, that they responded readily, even eagerly, to the

slightest show of interest on his part . . .
he knew, too, that Gemma had been
apprehensive rather than flattered—and he
appreciated that it must seem strange to
her that he should so abruptly be aware
of an appeal that he had never recognised
before.

He had always liked her, of course . . .
had always known a vague affection for the
girl. But it had never occurred to him
that affection could turn overnight into
something very much stronger—and he
wondered if it would ever have done so
if Crispin had not distressed Gemma and
therefore awoken his compassion and his
interest.

He was not so foolish as to suppose that
he had fallen in love with Gemma . . . he
distrusted emotions that flared to life too
rapidly. But he realised that she could
easily come to mean a great deal to him
—if he allowed it to happen. For the
moment, he accepted that she attracted
and interested and disturbed him more
than any woman had done since that disastrous affair in his early twenties: that she
had an enormous appeal for him that
might or might not develop into something

vital and lasting; that he had every intention of playing a bigger rôle in her life than he had done so far—and that it would be wise to proceed cautiously until he could be really sure how she felt about Crispin. He reminded himself that those feelings, however sincere, were doomed to disappointment in the circumstances—and he softly cursed Leonie for never having explained to her daughter that Crispin was also her child . . .

One day—which might not be very distant—Gemma was going to have to know the truth . . . and Adam Gantry made a silent vow then and there that he would be around at the time to put her small world to rights, to comfort and reassure her—and perhaps to clarify a dim realisation that Crispin was not the only man in the world who could love her and wish for her happiness.

He tossed his half-smoked cigarette through the window, turned the key in his ignition and started the car to make his way back to his home . . .

Gemma slipped up to her room, closed the door and stood with her back to the panels for a long moment, drawing a deep breath. She had never been so surprised in her life—that Adam of all people should suddenly react to her not only as a woman but as a kissable woman!

She touched her lips with gentle, hesitant fingers. Well . . . it had not really been a kiss, she reminded herself honestly —but the implication had been unmistakable! She had been thoroughly taken aback . . . had sat there like a stupid schoolgirl, silent and blushing, not knowing what to say or do. She wondered what he had thought about her lack of response, her seeming indifference to his touch and his nearness. Had he been annoyed with her? Disappointed? Or had it only been a small gesture of friendly comfort which was immediately dismissed from his mind. It had been impossible to gauge anything from his smile, his careless goodnight. She had not dared to turn back, to glance at him . . . she had scuttled into the house like a nervous, timid mouse, knowing that he was making no move to drive away and wondering why he should linger.

Had he only been sorry for her, trying to comfort her, she wondered, moving away from the door to stare at her reflection in the long mirror. She leaned closer to study herself. Was she so foolish as to imagine that he could possibly be attracted to her—that there was anything about her to which he could respond as a man does respond to a woman? Yet why not? Other men had paid her plenty of attention that evening . . . they had obviously found her attractive and worthy of their interest—and some of them had been quite as old as Adam. He was not really so old—and he disliked her thinking him too old for a girl of her age. Twenty-eight . . . almost twenty-nine—and she was eighteen. Lots of girls, some even younger than herself, went around with men in their late twenties and early thirties. She had listened to their chatter and gossip and speculation many times, heard them claim that older men were more considerate, more thoughtful, less selfish and irresponsible than younger men—and, without experience, she had listened without contributing to the conversation but privately thought that she would be terribly shy and nervous with any man other than Crispin.

Yet she was not shy of Adam. Not really

shy. That was probably because she had known him all her life. He was certainly more considerate and less selfish than Crispin . . . he was kind and reassuring and level-headed. He was not so much fun as Crispin, of course—but there were other things in life, more important things than having fun. Adam was adult and sophisticated—and Crispin, for all his appealing ways and good looks and easy charm, was still very much of a boy at heart . . .

Gemma reined her thoughts in sudden alarm. Good heavens! She was actually comparing Crispin with Adam almost to his detriment! Actually wondering what it might be like if Adam was her constant companion instead of Crispin! How . . . how *fickle*! It was bad enough that she had almost welcomed Adam's kiss, had almost encouraged him to seek her lips again, had almost reached out to draw him closer to her—but that she should dwell on what it might have been like if he had actually kissed her—and to dismiss the lovable, beloved Crispin as little more than an immature boy in comparison with his older brother!

It was only because she was hurt and unhappy that she was allowing herself to criticise Crispin, she assured herself—only because she was jealous of Bess. She could not really prefer to be courted by a man like Adam when she loved Crispin so much—with all her heart, she told herself emphatically. And she was leaping to ridiculous conclusions, anyway—she was making too much of a simple, affectionate, brotherly and very casual goodnight kiss that hadn't even been a proper kiss at all . . .

11

RESOLUTELY dismissing Adam from her mind, Gemma began to prepare for bed. Releasing her hair from its restraining pins, she brushed it as carefully and thoroughly as she did every night. She undressed, hanging her dress in the wardrobe, tidying her flimsy under-clothes, arranging her shoes neatly in their place—and slipped into the cool silk pyjamas.

She drew back the curtains and threw open the windows before getting into bed. Putting out the light, she nestled between the sheets—and thought of the noisy, lively crowd at the Hall, enjoying them-selves with a careless disregard of every-thing but having a good time. Her eyes smarted with sudden tears and she closed them tightly—she would not wallow in self-pity! Of course everyone was having fun . . . and she did not have to be in bed now, denying herself all opportunity of enjoying herself sufficiently to forget her heartache for a little while. Adam had been disappointed, she knew—and the knowledge was vaguely flattering. There had been so many pretty girls at the party, plenty of women only too willing to receive his attentions—but he had danced with no one but her, shown a heart-warming concern . . . and been rewarded for his efforts with the childish plea of a headache that was so obviously just an excuse to escape.

It had been silly to run away like that . . . it must have proved to Adam and everyone else that she was not nearly so adult as she would like to appear.

Adam had been prepared to devote himself to her for the rest of the evening —and it was just the kind of evidence she needed to convince Crispin and everyone else that she was indifferent to his neglect and capable of enjoying the company of another man. It would have been a feather in her cap to have Adam at her side while those other women envied and resented her for having apparently succeeded where they had failed. It wasn't just vanity . . . he was really very nice and he danced so well and he knew exactly how to make a woman feel that she was mature and attractive and self-assured. She had simply made a fool of herself and probably convinced Adam that she was not worth his interest—and it had been so silly to invent a headache when Crispin knew that she just never had headaches . . . and Adam really was charming and he'd been so kind and sweet . . . and perhaps she didn't love Crispin so much that she couldn't put it out of her mind and enjoy herself with Adam or someone else, her thoughts wandered with all the resilience of the very young as she drifted into sleep . . .

Leonie glanced at her daughter with a faint lift of an eyebrow as she slipped into her place at the breakfast table. Gemma looked well and very pretty with the faint flush of sleep touching her cheeks and her eyes bright enough to allay the anxiety of any mother's heart.

"How are you this morning? You left the party very early, didn't you . . . had you been drinking too much?"

"Oh, no, Mother," she replied quickly. "It was just a headache, really . . . the noise and the excitement, I expect."

Leonie's eyes narrowed. "Do you feel quite well?" she asked with swift concern . . . the child was flushed and perhaps her eyes were just a little too bright to be natural. "You don't usually have headaches—not sickening for something, are you?"

"Please, Mother . . . don't fuss!" Gemma almost snapped the words as she reached for bacon and kidneys and helped herself liberally with all the appetite of youth and health. She did not want to be reminded that her headache had been a mere fabrication . . . and she did not want her mother to probe into the motives for that pretence.

Leonie said nothing. Her lips tightened a little with annoyance as she reached for the coffee pot and filled Gemma's cup and her own.

Gemma knew and feared that stiff silence. She looked apprehensively at her mother, forgetting in that moment that she was supposed to have left childhood behind her, half-expecting to be sent back to her room in punishment for her rudeness.

"I'm sorry," she said tentatively. "I didn't mean to speak so rudely."

"Very well . . . we'll forget all about it." Leonie relented and smiled . . . the child was at a difficult age and everyone threw fits of temperament at times, she reminded herself. "What are you doing today, Gemma? Do you want to drive into Marchester with me?"

"There was some talk about spending the day at the Tarn . . . taking a picnic lunch," Gemma said quickly. "I expect Crispin will be telephoning soon. You don't mind, do you . . . it's so hot in the town this weather."

"Of course I don't mind—as long as you aren't going to be on your own all day. I don't expect to be back before dinner." Leonie pushed her chair back from the table and took a cigarette from the box. She turned it between her fingers before lighting it, glancing at Gemma a little hesitantly before saying: "I wasn't playing bridge the entire evening, you know . . . it struck me that Crispin wasn't paying you much attention. Are you sure that you'll be included in his plans today?"

Gemma concentrated on cutting a piece

of bacon so that she did not need to meet her mother's eyes. "Oh, I expect so . . . it isn't exactly Crispin's plan . . . it was just a general idea. I think quite a lot of people will be going."

"Well, I'm glad that you seem so unconcerned . . . I notice that he's just as light-hearted and fickle as he's always been. He was taking a great deal of interest in his cousin last night . . . as you claimed he would, if I remember rightly." She flicked a table lighter into flame and drew on her cigarette. "She's a pretty girl. Very well suited to him, I imagine. It might be an excellent thing if he were to settle down with one girl for a while . . . steady him, give him some sense of responsibility."

Gemma looked up, forcing a smile. "I can't imagine Crispin settling down with anyone for a long, long time. But he is fond of Bess . . . I think everyone must be. But you really shouldn't have worried, Mother—I've told you dozens of times that Crispin and I are only friends."

"Just as well," her mother said cryptically and rose to her feet, stubbing her unfinished cigarette. Abruptly she shot off on another tack: "I gather that Adam brought you home . . . unusual for him to be so attentive to you, isn't it? Or am I just out of touch?" She looked hard at her daughter as swift colour stole into her cheeks. "He's a little old for you, Gemma . . . why must you be so difficult, getting involved with all the wrong men. There are plenty of right ones about, after all."

"Oh, Mother!" Gemma protested instinctively, almost impatiently, resenting all this concern with what was in great measure her private affairs. "Adam brought me home out of kindness . . . I had a headache and wanted to come home and he knew you were enjoying your game of bridge. I don't suppose he was away from the party for more than ten minutes . . . and he certainly isn't interested in me, anyway. Are you going to ask the intentions of every man who pays a little attention to me? I'm not a child any more, you know."

Leonie smiled in faint sympathy with the protest—and she understood that it was justified. It had been unnecessary to mention Adam at all . . . it was just that she had been vaguely disturbed by Adam Gantry's unusual concern for Gemma when he was such an unemotional man, so seemingly indifferent to the opposite sex at all times. While it must be preferable for Gemma to be friendly with Adam rather than Crispin, he was still a Gantry—and there were plenty of men in the district who were not associated with that particular family by birth. Leonie could not suppress a faint sigh . . . it was all getting so difficult, so involved—she almost regretted that Gemma had not been told the truth about her mother's irrevocable connection with the Gantrys at a very early age. It might have been wiser if she had grown up with the knowledge . . . but it was too late now for regrets—and certainly not the right moment to blurt out that she had once been Philip Gantry's wife and that she was the mother of his youngest son!

So she said briskly: "No, you're no longer a child . . . men are bound to take notice of you. I shall have to curb my maternal instincts and trust you to discourage the wrong types. But it's very hard for a mother to admit that her daughter has any discrimination where men are concerned—and you are a little naïve, darling. I shall try not to interfere in future—but do remember that it's perfectly natural that I should worry about your happiness and peace of mind." She moved towards the door. "It's time I was leaving . . . I have an appointment at eleven. Enjoy your day, Gemma—and don't sit in the sun too much. That may have been the cause of your headache last night."

When her mother had gone, Gemma sat for some time at the table, replenishing her coffee cup and nibbling idly at a piece of toast.

She had spoken so lightly of joining the Gantrys on their suggested picnic and she supposed that they half-expected her to do so. She had been present when the idea was being discussed and it was taken pretty much for granted that she accompanied them on such expeditions. But Adam had not mentioned it again last night . . . and it was not likely that Crispin and Bess would welcome her company . . . or perhaps even notice whether she was present or not!

If she was pressed to join them she must be very careful not to make things difficult for Crispin she decided. It was true that he was not thinking of her feelings but that was no excuse for similar thoughtlessness on her part. After all, she had no claim on him. He was entitled to give his attentions to anyone he chose. And it was not his fault if he found Bess more attractive than the "girl next door."

She loved him . . . but she was not going to parade her love. She loved him— but it was all terribly hopeless and she had no choice but to conceal her feelings, to try to suppress them and to hope that one day she might meet another man that she could learn to love and who would love her in return.

The shrill summons of the telephone brought her instantly to her feet. Was it Crispin? Was he telephoning to ensure that she meant to go with them to the Tarn?

She could scarcely reach the telephone swiftly enough—and then she hesitated before lifting the receiver. If it was Crispin how should she speak to him? Should she be cool and casual—or just as friendly and eager as before? Supposing she was exaggerating his offhandedness of the previous day? Perhaps he had just behaved as he always did with a new flirtation—and it was only her new awareness of the way she felt about him that exaggerated his casual treatment out of all proportions! It was possible, she admitted to herself, realising how stupidly sensitive she had been of late, how jealous she had become of his friendship and affection.

She gave the number, a little breathlessly. "Gemma Gardner speaking," she added as she always did, knowing that people were apt to confuse her voice with that of her mother and rush straight into a long rigmarole about things that did not concern her.

"Adam here," he said easily. "How are you?"

She was not sure whether she was disappointed—or merely taken aback to hear his voice. She did not think that he had ever called her before—and her heart fluttered in slight alarm, this call following as it did on his unusual behaviour of the previous night.

"Oh, Adam . . ." she said blankly, foolishly. Then pulled herself together with an effort. "I'm fine—how are you?"

"Weary," he said and she could hear the

faint laughter in his tone. "That wretched party went on to the early hours and Crispin roused me out of bed ten minutes ago to remind me that we have a date at the Tarn. The frightening energy of the young! Will you be ready in half-an-hour . . . complete with swimsuit? It's going to be another scorcher, I imagine."

"I didn't know *you* meant to go on the picnic," Gemma said in surprise.

"Oh, I'm having a last fling before I settle down to old age," he said flippantly. "Do you mind—are you afraid that my presence will cast a damper on the high spirits of the younger members of the party?"

"Of course not!" Gemma protested. "I didn't mean that at all!"

Adam chuckled. "No headache this morning?"

Gemma blushed . . . even though he could not see the colour that swept into her cheeks. There was something in his tone that told her that he had not been in the least deceived by her fabrication—and that he had known and understood her reasons for wishing to leave the party so early. She did not resent his perception

. . . she was only faintly ashamed of her own weakness and cowardice.

"I feel fine," she assured him again.

"Good . . . I'll be over for you in half an hour."

He rang off abruptly—and Gemma, looking down at the burring receiver in her hand, wondered why he had called her. Was this more kindness on his part? Had Crispin seemed reluctant to include her in the picnic—and had Adam, knowing how she must feel if they left her out of their plans, decided to forgo the demands of his work so that he could be on hand to ensure her presence and her comfort? Or, incredibly, was he interested in her—enough to put the pleasure of a day in her company before the work he had never been known to neglect on two consecutive days?

He was coming for her in half an hour . . . and she did not know if she wanted to join the picnic party at all. For while she might appreciate the extent of Adam's kindliness, knowing in her heart that it could not be anything else, she was feminine enough to dislike his compassion and to be annoyed with herself for making it necessary. How foolish of her to betray her feeling for Crispin . . . how much more foolish to admit the truth to Adam so easily. She could have pretended complete indifference—if only she had not been so distressed at the time, so bewildered by the realisation that she loved Crispin and so hopelessly inexperienced in her handling of adult emotions.

Adam was kind and considerate—but it was scarcely flattering to any woman to know that a man's interest only stemmed from compassion and concern. And he was one man whose interest must be welcome to any woman—for he had never been prone to indulge in the light-hearted affairs that seemed so necessary to the other men she knew. If Adam Gantry was to seek a woman's company because he found her attractive and appealing then one could be sure that it was no light flirtation on his part. And that was something to admire and respect in a man, Gemma thought soberly—having been hurt and neglected too many times through Crispin's love of flirtation and having witnessed the unnecessary heartache and humiliation that was so often caused by light and meaningless affairs.

At eighteen, Gemma was much more inexperienced than most girls of her age . . . there had only ever been one man who interested her, whose company and attentions she welcomed—and she had allowed her life to revolve around the warm, comfortable friendship with Crispin Gantry. Perhaps she would have been wiser to have encouraged the occasional attentions of other men . . . to have accepted the occasional invitations that had come her way . . . to have played Crispin's own game, in fact.

Thinking deeply, she went up to her room to change . . . it might not be too late to salvage her pride after all . . .

Crispin took her for granted, of course . . . he had always done so. She had always been there when he wanted her . . . always been waiting without a word of reproach when he tired of the latest affair and turned to the easy, undemanding relationship he knew with her. He could not really be completely indifferent to the way she felt about him—and no man could have misread the love in her eyes, that naked revelation of all he had come to mean to her. He knew—of course he knew. But she had chosen the wrong time to realise that she loved him—and to betray it so unthinkingly. Just now he was in the throes of another flirtation—it could not be anything more than that—and he had been embarrassed and touched with a vague sense of guilt when he discovered that she loved him. But when he was over this infatuation for Bess then he would turn to her again, just as always . . . and surely that was proof that he cared more for her than he was prepared to admit at the moment. Perhaps he did not know that he loved her! Gemma had only just realised the truth for herself, after all.

And when he did tire of Bess . . . well, it would never do for him to find Gemma waiting patiently and unreproachfully once more. Crispin needed to be jolted into awareness of her importance in his life! And there was only one way to do it. She must pretend and convey an easy, light-hearted indifference to his new flirtation and an interest in someone else!

It was all so simple! Gemma wondered that she had not thought of it before—but, of course, it had never occurred to her before that she needed to resort to feminine strategy to secure Crispin's lasting and loyal affections.

She was not unattractive, she reminded herself—those men last night had hovered about her like moths to a candle flame, awakening her to the realisation of a power that she had not known she possessed. Any one among the young men she knew might be easily manoeuvred into the role of admirer—and encouraged into an affair that would prove to Crispin that she was not totally dependent on his friendship and companionship!

There was even Adam, she thought with a swift fluttering of excitement. He was almost playing into her hands. Perhaps it was her new power, her new and mature attraction for men, that had led him to attempt that kiss—and persuaded him that a day in her company would be more rewarding than the demands of the estate. It was surely possible. Even if he was not physically aware of her, if it was only kindness on his part, surely she could use that to her own ends? It might be unscrupulous —but no one else need know that he was only being kind or that she did not really feel warmed and flattered by his apparent interest.

It was certainly time she developed a little pride, anyway, she told herself sternly. The whole county must be aware of the long friendship between her and Crispin Gantry . . . must be aware of the many times he had deserted her for other girls . . . must be aware that she had never shown any interest in other men. She had invited her own humiliation . . . she would not do so again! She would give the county something else to think and talk about . . . and certainly there would be a buzz of speculation if she suddenly appeared to be Adam's girl instead of merely Crispin's friend. No one then could imagine her to be in love with Crispin or suffering at his hands . . .

12

GEMMA was waiting for Adam when he arrived—and she ran down the steps towards the car, swinging a gaily-striped towel in her hand, a cool primrose linen dress over her swimsuit and open-work primrose sandals on her feet.

"You look cool and fresh," he complimented, as she slipped into the car beside him. He was dressed with equal casualness in grey slacks and open-necked pale blue shirt—and he looked bronzed and masculine and remarkably handsome.

Gemma flashed him one of her lovely smiles. "I'm looking forward to a dip, though . . . I'm not as cool as I look." She leaned back in her seat, visibly relaxing, as the car slid away down the drive. "It must be some time since you went to the Tarn with us, Adam."

He nodded. "Too long, I expect. But I still know the way."

"I'm glad you decided to go," Gemma

told him lightly—and slipped her hand into the crook of his arm, determined to make a start on her new campaign.

If Adam was startled by her overture, he gave no sign. He turned his head to smile at her, hugged her hand against him for a brief moment . . . and then turned back to scan the long ribbon of road.

Gemma left her hand in his arm—and studied him thoughtfully but not too blatantly as they drove through the sunny countryside towards the Tarn. He was very handsome and there was a strength of character, a certain maturity, in his good looks that was lacking in Crispin's blond, masculine beauty. For the first time it occurred to her that while Adam and Balfour were easily identified as brothers, the Gantry looks were not quite so marked in Crispin. There was a likeness, of course . . . but he was blond where both Adam and Balfour were dark and his eyes were remarkably blue while Adam and Balfour had inherited the grey, steady, honest gaze of their father. She supposed idly that Crispin's colouring must have come from his mother—and all she or anyone else knew about Crispin's mother was that she had deserted husband and child soon after he was born. She was never talked about by the Gantrys or anyone else—and that wasn't really odd, Gemma told herself, remembering that it was ancient history ... over twenty years since it had all happened.

"Do you remember Crispin's mother?" she asked idly, following the trend of her thoughts.

Adam tensed briefly. "What an odd question!" he said as lightly as he could. "What put that into your mind?"

"I was just thinking of his colouring," she explained. "You and Balfour are so dark—and Crispin is unusually fair. Your features are alike, of course. I suppose he must be like his mother—and I just wondered if you could remember her at all. You're six years older than Crispin, aren't you?"

"Nearer seven," he returned carelessly. "His mother. . . ? I don't know that we saw very much of her at the time, Gemma —she was never particularly interested in children. I believe she was a blonde, though."

"I wonder why she ran away," Gemma

mused. "How could she leave your father and her dear little baby? How could any woman?"

Adam shrugged. "I expect she had her reasons . . . perfectly good ones from her point of view. The marriage was a mistake, I imagine—and I believe she didn't want to leave Crispin but my father insisted on having custody of him. You shouldn't think too badly of her, Gemma . . . neither you nor I know the whole story, after all."

"I don't think I've ever thought about her until now," Gemma told him lightly. "For years I believed he was Aunt Muriel's son, remember—and when I learned that he wasn't I wasn't really very curious. It never seemed important."

"And it does now?"

"Oh no! It was merely idle speculation."

He glanced at her, smiling. "Wondering if Crispin inherited his fickle ways from his mother?"

She coloured slightly. "It's possible, isn't it?" she demanded.

"His mother wasn't fickle . . . she married the wrong man, that's all. She married the other man, you know—and I don't suppose she's ever felt the slightest interest in another man since."

She was struck by something in his tone. She looked at him quickly. "Do you know her, Adam? Have you ever seen her since?"

He laughed. "What an odd child you are! Why on earth are you interested? Does it really matter who mothered Crispin—or what happened to her?"

"I suppose not," she agreed.

He turned off the main road into a narrow lane, driving slowly. "I expect the others have arrived," he said carelessly. "They left before I came to pick you up."

Gemma straightened in her seat and withdrew her hand from his arm to push back a stray tendril of her hair. She was a little apprehensive about the long day ahead of her . . . and she wondered if she could carry off the pretence as easily as she had supposed. She forgot that Adam had not really answered her question about Crispin's mother . . .

Adam parked the car beside the others, a little distance from the beautiful, secluded lake. By the time they had crossed the velvety grass to the place where the rest of their party had gathered, Gemma was prepared to play her part to the best of her ability.

Crispin was in the lake, streaking across the gleaming water with his blond head glinting in the sun: Bess and Balfour were treading water, talking and laughing and romping and they looked up as Adam called a greeting; Sandra Hamilton, Balfour's current girl-friend, was lying on her face on the thick grass, soaking up the sun, and talking idly to Muriel and Philip who had been easily persuaded to join the picnic party. There were several others in the water and reclining on the bank. . . men and girls well-known to Gemma who had attended the party on the previous night and been invited to join the party.

Gemma was conscious of raised eyebrows and curious glances as she arrived with Adam by her side, their hands lightly linked—and, clinging desperately to her self-possession, she glanced up at him, smiling warmly, and spoke to him with a faint tone of coquetry behind the words.

She greeted Crispin with careless warmth when he came, dripping with water, to throw himself on the grass by her side and rub his wet hair with a towel.

"How's the water?" she asked, smiling at him.

"Wet!" he told her, grinning. "Coming in?"

"Not yet . . . I will later."

Muriel was unpacking thermos flasks of coffee and Gemma went to help her. Crispin reached for his cigarettes and offered them to Adam who was idly plucking at a blade of grass. Philip was absorbed in a newspaper and they were a little distance from everyone else.

"Is she all right?" Crispin asked, jerking his head slightly in Gemma's direction.

"Of course," Adam said with a faint lift of his eyebrow.

"She came willingly."

"Why not? Don't make mountains out of molehills, Cris—she's used to your little ways by this time," Adam told him.

"I suppose so . . . but I don't want to make her miserable," Crispin said quietly, studying the end of his cigarette. "I'd better not be too offhand with her today . . . it might seem more noticeable in a smaller crowd."

"I doubt if Gemma would notice," Adam said, smiling softly. He was a very shrewd man—and he had sensed what lay behind the unusual friendship and warmth of Gemma's approach to him and he was quite prepared to support her in a little charade. She was being very sensible, he thought . . . it was much wiser to show unconcern and to allow people to believe that she was more interested in someone else than in Crispin. He did not mind that she had chosen him to be that someone else . . . it was just the way he wanted it. It might even turn out that a pretended interest developed into the real thing, given time and understanding and co-operation and encouragement . . .

That smile puzzled Crispin. He looked at his brother a little suspiciously . . . and his eyes narrowed further as Gemma came back to join them, carrying paper cups filled with steaming coffee, and Adam leaped to his feet to take them from her, smiling into her eyes with an expression in his own that Crispin had never seen him display to any woman before. Gemma looked up at him, responding to that smile as any woman would—and seeming more feminine and appealing in that moment than Crispin had realised she could be.

He was aware of a vast relief. He had never expected attraction to flare to life between Adam and Gemma—but now that it had happened he was not only relieved but gratified. Good old Adam . . . it was about time he relaxed and realised the pleasures to be found in a woman's arms —and Gemma was a lovely companion for any man who was not forbidden by ties of blood to appreciate her sweet charms to the full. Crispin had never been able to forget that Gemma was his half-sister—he had thanked heaven many times that she did not stir his senses as other women did. For some reason, she was simply not his type . . . But he could appreciate that other men would find her attractive and desirable—and he felt that Adam's sudden interest in Gemma could not have arisen at a better time. And Gemma was responding satisfactorily. Adam was a handsome man —one only had to watch the women who chased him quite blatantly to know that he was very attractive to them. It would be a good thing for Gemma to turn her thoughts and her emotions in another direction ... and it was a wonderful feeling to know that he no longer needed to worry about her, no longer needed to keep her at arm's length. He was so used to her ... knew all her moods and little ways ... he had missed the easy intimacy of their friendship, their mutual jokes, her infectious laughter and the vaguely flattering way she had of treating him as though he were only one step removed from a god. Now he could relax and behave normally.

He *had* imagined that look in her eyes, of course ... it had probably been meant for Adam and he had intercepted it by accident. Well, Adam could take care of himself—and for all Crispin knew, he welcomed the way things had turned out, might even be thankful that Gemma seemed to prefer him to his younger brother, after all. He wondered idly if it would come to anything ... there was no barrier to romance, even marriage, between them—Leonie Gardner might object to her precious child marrying any Gantry in the circumstances but she would have to tell Gemma her reasons and if Gemma was in love with Adam then she would not give a snap of her fingers for all that had happened in the past . . .

Remembering Adam's recent remarks and his light-hearted suggestion that he should sacrifice himself in a good cause, Muriel Gantry was more amused than surprised by the turn of events. She wondered idly if this rapidly-developing rapport was by mutual agreement—for she did not believe for a moment that the shy and immature Gemma could really appeal to Adam . . . or that the child would have the courage or the desire to throw out lures to the older, more experienced man who had always discouraged the advances of other women.

Her husband, apparently engrossed in his newspaper, was nevertheless sensitive to atmosphere and completely aware of all that was going on around him. He was rather baffled. He had been convinced that Gemma's affection for Crispin was only sisterly, that it would never occur to her to imagine herself in love with him. But now he was disturbed by the realisation that Gemma was throwing herself at Adam's head and he could only believe that it was a measure to arouse Crispin's jealousy and to punish him for paying so much attention to another girl. The child could not be aware that Crispin was too conscious of their undeniable relationship to be anything but relieved by her sudden interest in Adam.

Philip wondered if he had been wrong to laugh at Leonie's anxiety for her daughter's happiness. Leonie was the girl's mother, after all—if she had sensed danger in Gemma's preoccupation with Crispin then perhaps there had been sufficient danger to sense. There was no fear for Crispin's peace of mind . . . that was obvious. But Gemma had been kept in ignorance of the truth and perhaps it *was* possible that she could exaggerate her affection for Crispin into an imaginary love for him. Or perhaps into a very real love for him! Philip was suddenly as anxious about the girl's happiness as her mother. He hoped it was only the innocent and shortlived calf-love that was so likely at her age . . . he hoped that he might be completely mistaken about the whole thing.

But it was not like Gemma to treat Crispin with so much casual carelessness and to use all her feminine wiles on someone else in his presence. Adam must realise what she was doing . . . and yet he seemed to encourage it. Having forgotten that recent conversation with Muriel and his son, Philip could not even guess at Adam's motives—and he wondered if Adam, indifferent to women for so long, had finally succumbed to the dark and slender loveliness that even a man of Philip's age could well appreciate. If *he* realised that Gemma had never seemed so beautiful, so appealing, so abruptly mature as in the last few days, then was it so incredible that Adam might realise it too . . . and the man who did not indulge in light affairs was likely to fall very heavily when the right woman came into his life at the right moment . . .

Gemma was surprised to find how easy it was to charm a man into giving her his undivided attention. She did wonder if Adam had guessed her reasons for treating him almost as if he were the only person who existed for her on that picnic . . . but even if he had, he was co-operating and surely allaying anyone's suspicions where her feeling for Crispin was concerned. She was also surprised to realise that she was enjoying herself: it was a novel experience to have a man of Adam's calibre treating her with as much devotion and deference as though he had neither eyes nor thought for anyone else . . . and Crispin was being so much nicer to her than she had expected. Perhaps his infatuation for Bess was already wearing a little thin—or perhaps her tactics were already beginning to work. He was attentive to Bess, of course—but not to the point where anyone could remark on his neglect of Gemma or anyone else.

They swam, romping in the water like children with a great deal of laughter and squealing and shouting, their healthy bodies bronzed to golden tans by the long spell of hot, golden sunshine.

Gemma was an expert swimmer thanks to many hours of practice, many summers of swimming in the Tarn, the sea and the big open-air pool at the Country Club. The water was cold and clear and sparkling and was perfectly safe if one avoided the treacherous areas near the waterfall. The younger men delighted in scrambling on to the big rocks at the base of the waterfall and making their way, clinging to the slippery face, behind the rippling sheet of water and appearing again on the far side to dive into the lake, remaining out of sight long enough to bring throbs of anxiety to the less daring who watched before surfacing beside them like laughing seals.

Adam had outgrown such pranks but he could still be amused by them—and it gave him pleasure to see the bubbling merriment in Gemma's eyes and smile as she gave herself to the enjoyment of the fun as much as anyone else.

As if by some unspoken signal, everyone tired of the water and scrambled up to the grassy bank to throw themselves, panting and laughing and teasing each other, down on the thick velvety turf just as Muriel decided it was time to feed the hungry pack of young people.

Gemma munched sandwiches and hard-boiled eggs and drove white teeth into a chicken leg with a healthy, hungry appetite . . . and Adam studied her, smiling faintly. She did not look in the least like a girl who was fretting for her heart's desire . . . she was joining in the easy banter and laughing at the silly, youthful jokes and seemed to have completely forgotten her heartache.

After the picnic meal had been eaten and the remnants cleared away, everyone seemed sleepy. They lay around on the grass, talking desultorily, the laughter and banter dying down, content to enjoy the heat of the afternoon sun and the blissful relaxation after the exertion of their antics in the water and the satisfying of healthy appetites.

Adam closed his eyes: there had been few hours of sleep for him or anyone else on the previous night and he felt pleasantly weary. Gemma was lying on her stomach by his side, her head resting on her folded arms and her eyelids were drooping like a child's. He rolled over on to his own stomach, threw an arm about her shoulders and allowed himself to drift into drowsiness. The sun was warm on his bare back and he was vaguely conscious of the steady rhythm of her breathing. He heard the faint murmur of voices in the background, becoming fainter and fainter— and he must have slept for the next thing he knew was the annoying touch of a fly or some other insect about his face. He grunted and shifted his position, moving a hand to his face to brush away the insect —and he heard Gemma chuckle. He opened his eyes to find her leaning over him with a blade of grass in her hand.

Adam grinned and caught her wrist. "Infant," he reproached. "Lie down and go to sleep." He looked around him. His father was apparently fast asleep in his comfortable chair; Muriel was engrossed in the writing of a letter and she had turned her chair a little so that the sun was not directly on her; there was no sign of Crispin or Bess; Balfour and Sandra were lying close together, smoking cigarettes, talking in low, intimate tones and not in the least interested in anyone around them. They were some distance from any other members of the party.

He gave a little tug and Gemma, losing her balance, toppled to the grass beside him. He threw his arm about her again and drew her close to him.

"Go to sleep," he said again. "It's too hot for energetic games."

She lay on her back, looking up at him, her eyes dancing—and there was something very provocative in the tilt of her face, the expression in her violet eyes. He was suddenly fired with a desire that shocked him a little by its intensity. Perhaps it was her nearness, the tender curve of her breasts outlined by the clinging swimsuit, the dark strands of hair escaping from the pins to cling wetly about her throat, the proximity of those softly-parted lips and the hint of invitation in her eyes. But he wanted her then as he had never wanted any woman in his life—and even as he drew her fiercely into a hard, demanding embrace and kissed her with an urgent, almost angry passion, he knew that he loved her, that it was not just a physical urge that possessed him . . .

And Gemma, astonished, shaken, even a little frightened by the intensity of the emotion she had aroused in him, found that she was clinging to him, her arms about his lean body, her lips and body responding to him with a newly-awakened awareness of desire. Some imp of mischief had provoked her to tease him with that blade of grass, to rouse him from sleep, to look up at him with a faint challenge in her eyes . . . perhaps the impulse to know if that attempted kiss had been born of compassion or physical attraction. She would never need to wonder again if she was attractive to this man . . . this handsome, oddly exciting man whose kiss swept her unexpectedly and terrifyingly to the peak of a desire she had never experienced before.

He drew away, looking down at her with a strange expression in his grey eyes that she could not analyse . . . and she smiled, slowly, sweetly . . . put an arm about his neck and drew his head down to her once more . . .

13

B UT Adam merely brushed her lips fleetingly—and Gemma was filled with an angry disappointment. Then he released her, turned over and reached for his cigarettes.

Gemma sat up swiftly, putting up unsteady hands to her hair, not daring to look at him for fear she should meet his eyes and betray the sweet urgency which was clamouring in her body. Inexperienced though she was, she sensed that only a need for self-control had caused him to turn away from her so abruptly . . . and she realised for the first time to what extent a woman has power over a man.

She thought of Crispin and knew that despite the fact that she loved him, she could not imagine herself wanting to be kissed so passionately by him or imagine her body responding so swiftly and fiercely to his kiss. There had never been any physical force in her feeling for Crispin . . . but with a new shrewdness she realised that just because Adam's kisses could rouse her to passion it did not mean that she had to be in love with him. She was not yet ready to accept that her lack of physical desire for Crispin implied that her feeling for him could not really be love . . . after all, he had never kissed her as a man kisses a woman, had never held her in his arms in that ardent embrace, had never tensed at her touch or looked at her with just that fierce flame in his eyes. Perhaps if she could tempt Crispin into kissing her, as she had consciously and unashamedly tempted Adam, she would know once and for all if she loved Crispin as a woman loves a man . . .

Adam glanced at her, vaguely suspicious of the thoughts that touched her violet eyes. "What mischief are you brewing now, infant?" he asked, his voice steady now, his body eased of its hunger and trembling, his heart and mind aware that he needed caution in his dealings with Gemma as he had never needed it before.

She shook her head. "Nothing. . . Adam, do you think anyone saw us?" she asked, a little hesitantly, suddenly conscious of embarrassment and nervousness for fear her mother should hear about her brazen lovemaking with Adam Gantry.

"Does it matter?" he asked carelessly. "I imagine everyone believed it to be inevitable. Do you mind what people might say?"

"No, I suppose not," she said slowly.

Adam chuckled. "Yes, you do—but you aren't a fallen woman just because I kissed you in full view of anyone who was interested enough to watch. Anyway, you wanted to be kissed—didn't you?" he added with a note of mocking challenge in his voice.

He was amused when faint colour stole into her cheeks . . . amused and touched by her youth and innocence—and thankful to the depths of his being that she was so innocent and untouched and vulnerable.

"Only to find out what it was like!" Gemma retorted a little defensively.

Adam raised an eyebrow in astonishment. He could not be the first man to have kissed her, surely! And yet it was true that she had never bothered with any man but Crispin . . . and he was the last person in the world to have even thought of kissing her!

He smiled at her tenderly, put out a hand to touch her cheek with gentle fingers. "And what is it like?" he asked softly, watching the colour deepen until it touched the roots of her hair—and wanting to kiss her again with every fibre of his being, loving her as he had never believed he could love any woman.

Gemma glanced at him provocatively, impishly, beneath the thick veil of her lashes. "Nice," she said, laughter bubbling in her voice.

"Is that all—just 'nice'?" he demanded in mock indignation.

"Well, it was only one kiss," she reminded him mischievously. "It's difficult to judge . . . perhaps if you were to kiss me again. . . ?"

"I will—but not here, not now," he told her, amusement flickering about his mouth. He caught her slim, brown hand in his own and lifted it to his lips turning it to kiss her palm. He longed to tell her that he loved her, that he wanted to marry her, that she was now and always the most important part of his life—but he restrained the impulse. It was much too soon . . . and even though she had responded so sweetly, so wonderfully to his kiss it did not need to mean anything but a new awareness of passion. He did not dare to delude himself that she could have given her heart as rapidly, as lastingly as he had given his to her. He did not dare to hope that his kiss had stamped out the mild, innocent feeling for Crispin that she had glorified by the name of love . . . it might be possible for her to love a man who had never held her, never kissed her, never murmured endearments against her lips, never stirred her to desire with his kiss and his touch and his nearness. He doubted it but he could not know . . .

He was thankful that the shy, inexperienced, very young girl was not ill at ease with him since that kiss . . . she might so easily have been and then he would have known that it was hopeless for him to love her, to want her, to believe that one day she might love him and be happy to spend the rest of her life with him. She had teased him like any adult woman. . . invited him openly to repeat the experience—and surely she could not now believe herself in love with Crispin? No woman could welcome or want another man's kisses if she was in love—and she would not respond as Gemma had responded. He had half-expected a rebuff ... but not that warm, sweet urgency of lips and body and blood which had almost swept him into ecstacy. She was young and ardent and bewitching—and he told himself that if he ever won her love they would need to marry without delay. No man, no woman, could withstand the fierce desire of such love-making for long without throwing all caution to the four winds.

He was glad that he loved her ... glad that he could claim with complete honesty that this was not just physical attraction. He loved her too much, too tenderly, too protectively to doubt the purity and integrity of this new emotion which had invaded his heart and his life. He could not know if she would ever love him ... but deep within him there was a conviction that would not be denied that inasmuch as she was the only woman for him, he was the only man for her although she was as yet unaware of the fact.

It did not occur to Gemma to be shy, to feel embarrassed . . . that kiss had come about so naturally, so joyously even if she had half-consciously manoeuvred it. She did not know that he loved her . . . such a thought did not even cross her mind. But she was comforted by a strange assurance that his interest in her was not born of mere kindness and compassion, after all. He thought of her as a woman—and she had become truly a woman in his arms. The last vestiges of immaturity had slipped away from her heart and mind—and she was born into a new self-possession that sat on her shoulders so easily that she might never have lacked it.

She looked at Adam with a strange warmth about her heart . . . and she wanted to reach out and touch him, gently, a little possessively, as though she was claiming her own before the world. The impulse was in her heart and mind and body . . . but she did not realise why she wanted the reassurance of touch, why she wanted him to return her gaze with that certain look in his eyes, why she wanted him to turn to her with a smile that was only for her, that he must never, ever give to another woman. These were all new feelings for Gemma . . . and she was not ready yet to analyse them. This was the real dawn of delight that Adam had talked about—if only she had known it just then. This was the first stirring of a love that was to possess her completely, to alter her entire life, to last till eternity . . . the dawn of a delight that only Adam and his love could bring to fulfilment, the promise of a happiness that only Adam could bring to her heart and mind—and for the moment it was just a vague stirring, a vague dissatisfaction for all that did not seem to exist between them, a vague yearning that she was too hesitant to define . . .

Philip stirred in his chair, opened his eyes, yawned and stretched and grinned a little sheepishly as he realised their glances . . . and the spell was broken. He straightened in his chair and Muriel turned from her letter-writing and Balfour called across to his brother . . . and then everyone was astir and talking at once and another dip in the lake was suggested just as Crispin and Bess returned from their walk . . .

"Well, my child—did you enjoy the

day?" Adam asked as he brought the car to a halt outside the Manor House.

Gemma turned to him eagerly. "Of course . . . it was a lovely day. Are you glad you went instead of working on those stuffy old books or tramping over the estate and talking to dreary farmers?"

"I enjoy my stuffy old books and some of those dreary farmers are great friends of mine," he told her lightly. "But I'm glad I took a holiday," he added, smiling at her indulgently.

"Are you coming in for a drink?" she invited.

"No, thanks. I must get home . . . I have to change, reserve a table at the Country Club and be on time for my appointment with a very lovely girl."

Gemma felt an odd little pang in the region of her heart. "Oh . . . I see," she said, her voice stiff with the need to conceal her chagrin. And she had imagined that he had little interest in women . . . that he was truly attracted to her! She was suddenly angry with herself for attaching so much importance to a mere kiss.

Adam could not have wished for a more gratifying reaction to his teasing words.

227

But while he was thankful to notice the faint shadow that crossed her face, he could not bear to let her suffer even the slightest hint of disappointment. "Be ready at seven, infant," he told her sternly. "You're young enough not to have learned the stupid trick of keeping a man waiting."

Her eyes glowed with pleasure. "Do you mean *me?* You're taking *me* to the Country Club?"

He leaned over to kiss her . . . hard and swift. "Of course . . . I mean to make the most of my holiday," he said, smiling . . .

Gemma ran down the wide staircase, her eyes shining, her dark hair gleaming with much use of the brush and piled high on her head, glowing from her bath and emanating a soft, delicate perfume as she moved.

Leonie, still dressed in the immaculate linen suit she had worn all day, looked up in surprise from her magazine as her daughter came into the sitting-room. It was not difficult to detect a faint excitement in Gemma's mood . . . and she was looking lovelier, if that was possible, than she had on the previous night.

"Well!" she exclaimed, amusement touching her words. "For whose benefit is all this beauty—or shouldn't I ask? Not for an evening at home, I'm sure."

Gemma laughed softly. "Adam is taking me to the Country Club. I won't be too late, Mother."

"Adam? Adam Gantry?" Leonie could not hide her astonishment . . . or her concern. "Darling, I do hope you aren't getting involved . . ."

Gemma broke in on the words. "Mother, you promised not to interfere," she reminded her lightly with the easy self-possession of her new maturity. She was suddenly no longer awed or frightened by her mother—and she smiled at her affectionately, thinking of her as another woman for the first time in her life.

Leonie nodded slowly but a shadow touched her eyes. Now she knew that her daughter was grown-up, that the old relationship had subtly altered and would never be the same again, that in future Gemma would owe more love and loyalty to someone else than she owed to her mother—and while she was aware of a new affinity with the girl who smiled at her with the eyes of a woman, she was moved to sadness by her innocent eagerness to cross the threshold of maturity with all its attendant griefs and burdens and anxieties which could only become worthwhile if one was blessed with the happiness and comfort and peace of mind of loving and being loved by the right man.

"You're old enough to know what you're doing," she said quietly, generously and checked the words of caution that hovered on her lips. She lifted her cheek for Gemma's light kiss. "Have a nice time, darling."

Gemma heard the sound of the car and flew to the window. "He's here!" she exclaimed eagerly. "Shall I ask him in for a drink, Mother?"

"Not tonight, dear . . . I've only just come in and I feel too tired for small talk. Another night . . ."

Gemma did not attempt to persuade her. She blew her mother a kiss . . . and went from the room, slipping her wrap about her shoulders.

Leonie rose and walked to the window, watched as Adam stepped from the car to greet Gemma with a smile and a clasp of his hand that spoke volumes to the mother who knew so much more of life and love than it was possible for Gemma to know.

She sighed. She did not know how it had happened but Adam Gantry was in love with Gemma, her little girl, her beloved child . . . and Gemma was either cock-a-hoop with this unexpected conquest or on the verge of being in love with *him*.

She did not know whether to be glad or sorry. She was both relieved and thankful that Gemma had not fallen in love with Crispin, after all . . . at the same time, she wished that her daughter were not so obsessed with the Gantrys. Not content with avoiding the danger of loving Crispin, she had decided to risk her heart in the hands of Adam Gantry. Leonie had nothing against Adam . . . she had always liked him, considered him to be the finest of Philip's three sons—even above her own son. But if Gemma fell in love with Adam and wanted to marry him, she would have to know the truth about her mother and Crispin. Well, she would have to cross that bridge when she came to it, Leonie decided, dismissing the thought of that unpleasant duty as she had done so many times in the past . . .

That evening set the pattern for others and while Adam was too conscientious, too absorbed in his work on the estate to neglect it more than occasionally, he spent almost every moment of his free time with Gemma . . . and became more deeply in love with every moment.

She was happy in his company, conscious of the tenderness and affection and warmth with which he surrounded her, delighting in the knowledge that it was swiftly accepted by everyone that Adam Gantry was courting her while Crispin remained as devoted to Bess as though he intended to settle down at last.

Gemma found that she was no longer distressed by Crispin's preference for the other girl . . . she could even accept that Bess was much more suited to him than she had ever been. But still, at the back of her mind and deep in her heart, lingered a vestige of her feeling for him—and she knew that there was only one way to destroy it for ever or to give it new and lasting life. He had never kissed her, never held her in his arms—and now that she knew that a man's kiss could evoke a swift mounting of desire she wanted Crispin to kiss her with an almost desperate intensity. If he could stir her blood as Adam had done that day . . . then she would know that she loved him. It seemed foolish even to Gemma . . . but she knew she could never be sure until she had achieved that one kiss from a man who continued to treat her with a brotherly affection.

And Adam, loving her, sensing her every thought and feeling, knew exactly what lay behind her reluctance to give her heart to him . . . and could not conceive how matters could ever be resolved. Crispin would never feel the desire to kiss her . . . and thus Gemma would never be sure in her own heart that she did not love Crispin. He did not know how he knew what was in her mind and heart for she had never betrayed it . . . but he did know and it disturbed him. At the same time he kept a tight rein on his own passions and emotions, never allowing himself to betray that he loved her, never kissing her except lightly and briefly, showing her affection and warmth and tenderness but reluctant to sway her uncertain emotions with passion. He wanted her love . . . not just the swift leaping of a desire to match his own. And she would never love him while she wondered if her feeling for Crispin verged on the maturity of the love that a woman could know for a man who also stirred her blood with his embrace . . .

The days slipped by and drifted into a week and then a fortnight. And each day that passed left Gemma with the same uncertainty, the same desperate need to know, the same unfulfilled longing for just one kiss from the man who had never put an arm about her except in affection, who had never murmured an endearment into her ear or smiled at her with that special warmth which assured a woman that she was loved, who had never kissed her except in friendship on her birthdays and special occasions.

But Crispin's birthday was drawing near . . . and a party was planned to celebrate it. Not a big, noisy, crowded party such as the Gantrys loved to give but a small, intimate affair. Crispin had plans of his own for the day . . . the intention to announce his engagement to Bess . . . and, because he was very young at heart and loved secrets like any boy, he had urged Bess into a promise that no one should know of the engagement until he announced it himself at his birthday party.

As Gemma dressed for the evening, she told herself that this occasion might be her last opportunity to claim the kiss that he always gave her on his birthday—or her own. Anything could happen before her next birthday dawned . . . and it was a whole year before he would have another. It was an opportunity that she must use to full advantage . . . and she did not intend that kiss to take place in full view of everyone.

She dressed with special care, donning a new dress of flame-coloured velvet that clung to her lovely figure, slipping diamond studs in her ears and a diamond clip in her dark hair, taking careful pains with her make-up and dabbing perfume on her wrists and her throat. She was learning rapidly, she thought with a faint smile—learning the gentle art of seduction and it would not be her fault if Crispin could resist the temptation of her eager lips and provocative invitation of eyes and voice and smile . . .

14

IT was late in the evening before Gemma noticed that Crispin had left the big room where everyone was gathered. He had slipped through one of the windows that led to the terrace.

He was alone: Bess was talking to her mother and Muriel; Adam was providing fresh drinks for the party and she had just returned from renewing her lipstick and perfume and securing her dark hair more firmly.

No one noticed, she was sure, as she turned and slipped out of the room. If they had they would only believe that she had forgotten something . . . no one had reason to suspect that she wished to be alone with Crispin. She went along the hall to the library, crossed the room to the terrace. Crispin was smoking a cigarette and gazing across the shadowed gardens. He turned eagerly at the sound of her steps . . . and Gemma knew that he had expected Bess.

She joined him, smiling up at him, careful to seem at ease. "Isn't it a marvellous night? You've always had good weather on your birthdays . . . that's the advantages of being a summer baby, I suppose. I wonder if it was a night like this when you were born."

"I never had the chance to ask my mother," he said carelessly.

She put a hand on his arm. "Oh, I'm sorry, Crispin . . . I didn't mean to hurt you." She looked up at him in gentle concern. "Were you . . . thinking about her—out here on your own?"

He laughed. "Lord no! Why should I? She doesn't mean a thing to me . . . the only mother I've ever had is Muriel and I wouldn't have it any different." He looked at her curiously. "What on earth made you curious about the night I was born, anyway?"

She gave a little shrug . . . and her perfume wafted on the cool night air. "I don't know . . . perhaps I was remembering other birthdays—when we were children. It seems such a long time ago."

Crispin grinned. "Oh, we're not that old, Gemma. I can remember some of them very well . . . we had a lot of fun, didn't we?"

She moved a little closer to him—not too obviously. "This must be the first birthday that you haven't had a kiss from me, Crispin," she said lightly, smiling. "Are we too old for such things, do you think?"

He slipped an arm about her shoulders in the old gesture of affection. "Haven't I kissed you? You must be the only one . . . where were you when that little ceremony was being carried out?"

"Oh, I was there," she admitted, a little shyly. "But it seemed such a family thing . . . I don't know. So many things have changed since we've grown up, Crispin."

His arm tightened. "Don't be silly, my sweet—you *are* family," he told her warmly. He put a hand beneath her chin and tilted her face and brought his head down to kiss her . . . and Gemma slipped her hands about his neck and gave him her lips with a fierce passion that stunned and horrified him.

His lips were cold and unyielding—and he forced her away from him with angry hands. Gemma stared at him, the pain of rejection ripping through her—and she shrank from the cold fury in his very blue eyes. Something stirred in her . . . a memory, a faint realisation, a dim horror.

"Don't you ever do that again!" he said quietly—but his tone was harsh and again that strange sensation of familiarity sent her mind scurrying from all it implied.

"But, Crispin . . ." she began, almost in tears.

"But me no buts," he broke in in a tone that froze her to the depths of her being. "I've told you—no more of it, Gemma." He turned away from her abruptly. "It's . . . it's disgusting! Oh my God—go back into the house, will you! Leave me alone!" The sudden storm of emotion shocked her more than his harshness—and she backed away, frightened, bewildered, as he buried his face in his hands.

"Crispin . . ." She whispered his name. Almost put out her hand to touch him— and then the shock of his revulsion from her very presence hit her with such force that she could only turn and run—without even knowing where she meant to go.

Adam caught her by the shoulders, steadied her as she rocked with the unexpected impact, looked for a long moment into her distraught face and then drew her into his arms with a great tenderness.

"My poor darling," he murmured as she stood shuddering in his arms. "My love . . . my little love, don't run away from me," he pleaded as she struggled and fought to escape.

"He . . . he hates me," she sobbed, bitter tears coursing down her cheeks.

"No," he soothed. "No—you must never think that, my darling."

She clung to him suddenly, seeking reassurance. "Adam, Adam—hold me! *You* love me, don't you—say that you love me! You wouldn't shrink from me as he did . . . turn away so you wouldn't have to look at me! What have I done . . . what did I ever do?"

He stroked her hair, kissed the salt tears from her cheeks with infinite love in the touch of his lips. "Hush, my love. . . hush —you don't understand, you don't know . . . he doesn't mean to hurt you, he loves you—but not in the way you want."

"Why not? Why is it so impossible? What's wrong with me?" she cried out of her pain.

He held her closer, loving her more than he had ever loved her—and he had thought that to be impossible. "Nothing that you can help . . . or that we can alter, my darling," he said softly.

She quietened, stood still in his arms, looking up at him to scan his face with a new alertness. "Then there is a reason . . . a good reason? And you know what it is?"

"Yes . . . I know."

"Then tell me . . . Adam, I have to know," she pleaded.

"I haven't any right to tell you," he returned slowly, regretfully.

"Then I'll ask Crispin—make *him* tell me!" She moved to wrench herself from his arms.

He held her firmly. "He probably would poor devil . . . he's always wanted you to know. But he hasn't the right either—and you mustn't ask him, Gemma."

"I don't understand all this mystery!" she cried in anguish.

"I never understood the need for it, either," he said grimly.

She stared at him, baffled, bewildered —and then, studying him so intently, she was reminded again of Crispin's blond hair in comparison with the crisp darkness of Adam's colouring, of those very blue eyes that always seemed to hold the promise of a smile . . . and she thought of that strange something in his eyes, that strange familiarity in his voice, the strange tightening of his mouth which had reminded her of someone else . . . someone else . . . someone with his colouring, with eyes that could promise a smile and yet be so cold and steely, with a mouth that could be warm and generous and tighten into grimness so abruptly, with a voice that was husky and rich and yet could ring so frighteningly with harshness—and suddenly everything fell into place.

And she could only look at Adam with that new knowledge in her eyes . . . a look so full of pain and accusation and realisation that it was hard for him to meet it without flinching.

"You knew," she said slowly. "You knew . . . and he knew . . . and everyone knew—but no one ever thought to tell me. Not even my mother! She's *his* mother, isn't she . . . the woman you didn't want to talk about . . . the woman you wouldn't condemn because she left her husband and baby for another man? My mother—and Crispin's mother . . . oh, how horrible." And she shuddered at the memory of her willingness to give Crispin her lips, her obsession with the desire for his kiss, her foolish belief that the only man she could ever love was—her own brother!

"No, you didn't know," he comforted her gently. "No one could blame you for thinking that you loved him." He brushed his lips against her dark hair. "But it's over now . . . nothing can hurt you now. You know the truth—and you never loved him." He shook her a little roughly, his hands gripping her shoulders. "You never loved him, my darling," he said again with quiet urgency, knowing that he must impress it on her mind and heart or she would live with a sense of guilt for the rest of her life.

She looked up at him for a long moment, her eyes dark with pain and bewilderment . . . and then a long sigh rippled through her slender body—and she relaxed against him. "No, I never did," she said . . . so softly that he scarcely caught the words.

"So it doesn't matter who or what he is, does it?" he urged gently.

Gemma scarcely heard him . . . she was too busy with her thoughts, realising that everything was falling into place, that things that had once mystified her were now explained, knowing why her mother had never liked her close association with Crispin or his family once she passed from childhood to adolescence. She should loathe and despise her mother . . . but she could not. She remembered Adam's calm reminder that no one should judge anyone else . . . that the heart had its own reasons. And because she was a woman, so newly matured, and gaining a new understanding of adult emotions, she was very near to an understanding of her mother's love for a man who was not her husband and her reasons for keeping the truth from the daughter she loved and whose love and respect and admiration she needed so desperately. She could even appreciate a little that a woman could leave behind the baby son who had not been born of mutual love. They were only vague, bewildered perceptions . . . but the very fact that she could sense these things at all was evidence

that she had lost every vestige of her childhood and immaturity.

Crispin walked towards them, hesitantly, seeking his brother's eyes . . . and
Adam nodded. Gemma stiffened, hearing
the footsteps and sensing the presence of
the man who had been her dear friend, her
constant companion, the nearest thing she
had known to a brother, for so many
years.

She loved him dearly—and she knew
him too well to doubt his grief and his
anguish. She released herself from Adam's
arms and turned to face Crispin . . .

The man and the girl looked at each
other for a long moment . . . and then
Gemma held out her arms to him, smiling
through tears, and they held each other
close in the warm, tender embrace of
brother and sister who had shared all the
fun and adventure and joys and small
griefs of growing up together.

Breaking away, they smiled at each
other in affection . . . and then Adam took
Gemma's hand in his own and looked
down at her with his heart in his eyes. And
Crispin sensed that he was no longer there

as far as they were concerned . . . and he hurried away in search of his own love . . .

Gemma smiled mistily. "Kiss me," she said softly.

Adam chuckled softly. "You and your kisses . . ." he teased as he took her into his arms and touched her hair, her closed eyelids, her cheek and the corner of her mouth with his lips before her lips parted eagerly, ardently beneath his own. Time stood still . . . and when he lifted his head Gemma knew without a shadow of doubt in heart or mind that there was only one man in the whole world who possessed all the love she could give.

There was no need for mutual declarations . . . they knew without words that their love for each other would bind them irrevocably for the rest of their lives . . .

We hope this Large Print edition gives you the pleasure and enjoyment we ourselves experienced in its publication.

There are now more than 2,000 titles available in this ULVERSCROFT Large print Series. Ask to see a Selection at your nearest library.

The Publisher will be delighted to send you, free of charge, upon request a complete and up-to-date list of all titles available.

Ulverscroft Large Print Books Ltd.
The Green, Bradgate Road
Anstey
Leicestershire
LE7 7FU
England

GUIDE
TO THE COLOUR CODING
OF
ULVERSCROFT BOOKS

Many of our readers have written to us expressing their appreciation for the way in which our colour coding has assisted them in selecting the Ulverscroft books of their choice. To remind everyone of our colour coding— this is as follows:

BLACK COVERS
Mysteries

*

BLUE COVERS
Romances

*

RED COVERS
Adventure Suspense and General Fiction

*

ORANGE COVERS
Westerns

*

GREEN COVERS
Non-Fiction